BLOOD SAGA

Blood Saga

Preston Lewis

THORNDIKE PRESS
A part of Gale, a Cengage Company

LIBRARY OF CONGRESS CIP DATA ON FILE.
CATALOGUING IN PUBLICATION FOR THIS BOOK
IS AVAILABLE FROM THE LIBRARY OF CONGRESS.

ISBN-13: 978-1-4328-9859-5 (hardcover alk. paper)

Published in 2022 by arrangement with Preston Lewis.

Printed in Mexico
Print Number: 01   Print Year: 2022

For Barb and Garey Ketcham,
fine folks and good friends
from Wyoming

PROLOGUE

When she glanced up from the handkerchief she was trimming with a lace border, Mary Child caught her breath. Three men were riding up the gulch, aiming straight for the modest cabin she called home.

Just beyond the edge of the narrow porch, her four-year-old son, Virgil, was digging in the dirt with a rusty spoon he had found somewhere about the place. Glancing up from his tiny excavations and spotting the riders, Virgil jumped to his feet and scurried to his mother, grabbing her skirt and trembling.

"Rueben," Mary called to her husband as she stabbed the pure white handkerchief with her needle, "we've bad company approaching."

Rueben looked up from the bridle he was repairing. "They ain't Apaches, so they ain't

7

bad," he chided. "You worry too much, Mary."

Maybe so, Mary thought, but just the day before she had spotted these riders exploring the stream through the gulch. Rueben had seen them, too, but had told her not to worry, for they were only watering their horses. Many times Rueben had soothed her nerves since they had moved into the broad valley between the Jicarilla Mountains to the north and the Sacramento Mountains to the south. Rueben, who dreamed of building a ranching empire, was a good, honest and trusting man. And, a hard worker. While others were rustling cattle or prospecting for minerals, Rueben figured to make a decent living for his family by starting a small herd of cattle and ranching. His wasn't the best ranch land in the territory, but it wasn't the worst either. It had water and acceptable grass, but most of all it had Rueben Child, who would irrigate it with his sweat.

"Want me to get your pistol?" Mary offered as she arose from her rocker. She felt an uneasiness in her stomach as she watched the riders drawing nearer. Virgil, too, was nervous, his dirty fingers clinging to the folds of her skirt.

"Quit your worrying, Mary," Rueben

replied as he stood up from his stool at the end of the porch and slipped to his wife's side. He kissed her softly on the cheek and his free hand made a pass through his son's hair. Virgil giggled at his father's touch, then fell silent as Rueben stepped to a peg in the wooden doorframe where his pistol hung.

Mary was glad he had decided to take the pistol, but her hopes faded when he merely hung the bridle over his holster and stepped off the porch to greet the three riders. She was so scared, yet Rueben was so brave. Or, trusting!

"They may want a bite to eat, nothing more, Mary."

"We don't have much, just some cold taters and hard bread."

Rueben nodded. "Put some back for Virgil. We can give them the rest and send them on their way so you won't be so edgy."

Mary retreated inside, dragging Virgil, his fist knotted in the folds of her skirt, with her. She put the unfinished handkerchief on the table by the pen and inkwell. She glanced at the pan on the stove and saw four boiled potatoes, enough for the visitors with one left over for Virgil, and half a loaf of bread. She didn't mind doing without supper as long as Virgil had something to eat, and as long as the riders went away.

At her feet, Virgil fretted yet. Mary moved behind the table so she could see the three men as they reined up in front of her husband. For a moment, nobody said a thing as they sized each other up. Mary felt her nerves tightening at the sight of their eyes brimming with meanness and their lips curling with hate. Maybe their scowls were caused by hunger, but if they needed food, why hadn't they approached the cabin the day before?

"Afternoon, fellows," Rueben said. "Need a bite to eat before you ride on? Rueben Child is my name."

The three men exchanged sinister smiles and one, a tall, lean man with red hair, took off his hat and leaned forward in his saddle. "I'm Ed Keller," he announced.

Mary grabbed the pen from the inkwell and looked for a sheet of paper. She must write their names down and carry the list to the sheriff her next trip to Lincoln. Fearing Virgil had taken the paper during his play, she gritted her teeth and wrote Keller's name on the handkerchief, ruining the cloth she had been trimming in lace.

"This here's Van McCracken and Tom Long," Keller announced.

Mary wrote furiously on the handkerchief, adding both names.

"Whose place is this?" Keller asked.

"Mine," Rueben replied, "and you're welcome to water in the stream and food, but we don't have room to give you a bed with a roof over it."

Keller toyed with his hat as he looked around. "A cabin's about all you got here, not even a corral for your horse." He pointed with his hat at Rueben's hobbled mare grazing fifty yards away.

"I started small," Rueben said without shame.

Keller nodded. "Me and my boys figure we want to find us a place where we can start small and build our fortunes, too."

Rueben nodded. "Plenty of government land still available."

Keller replaced his hat on his head. "Yes, sir, I'm sure there is, but me and the boys had our hearts set on this place."

Crossing his arms over his chest, Rueben shook his head. "It ain't for sale."

Mary saw the other two men lick their lips.

Keller shook his head. "We weren't figuring to buy it, maybe trading for it, say another piece of land."

"Can't do it," Rueben said. "I figure on —"

Before he could finish, Mary saw the three men jerk their pistols. Dropping the pen, she clutched the handkerchief to her bosom and screamed. She knocked Virgil down as she lunged for the door. The pistols exploded and Virgil wailed at the sound of the booming guns.

Rueben clutched at his chest, then stood a moment before collapsing upon the ground.

Mary dashed off the porch, crying as she ran. "Why, why, why?"

The smell of gunpowder stung her nose and her eyes overflowed with tears. For a moment, she forgot everything but her husband, crumpled upon the ground before her. She fell to her knees beside him, but Virgil's crying caught her attention and she turned toward the cabin, where her son stood in the door, tears running down his cheek. As his eyes met hers, Virgil rushed toward her, stumbling off the porch and throwing himself in her arms. He buried his head in her breast and sobbed in terror.

She turned and glared at the three men. "Why, why?"

"Nothing personal, ma'am," Keller said, reholstering his pistol, then taking off his hat again. "We just wanted your land."

"There's plenty of land for the taking in New Mexico Territory."

"We had our reasons," Keller replied.

The one named Long waved his pistol at

Virgil. Instantly, Mary grabbed her son and shielded him from the bad men. "Are me and my son next?"

Keller shook his head. "We don't kill women and children."

"You just killed an unarmed man," Mary shot back.

"Let's kill 'em," Long scowled, "or they'll tell the law."

Keller twisted around and shook his head at Long. "You ain't got a decent streak in you, Tom. Put up your gun." Keller turned back to Mary. "You best be getting your man's horse and riding away from here or we might reconsider. And if you tell the law, you and your boy are as good as dead."

"I'm not leaving until I bury my husband." Mary wanted to cry, but knew it would only frighten Virgil more.

"Suit yourself," Keller said, dismounting and dropping his reins to the ground. He sauntered to Rueben Child's body. "Good shooting, boys." The other two nodded, then laughed.

Virgil lifted his head from his mother's breast, glanced at his dead father, then hid his eyes again.

With handkerchief in hand, Mary leaned over her husband's body and dipped the clean cloth into each of the three bloody wounds in his chest.

The three killers seemed transfixed by her action.

"What's that for?" Keller asked.

"It's for my boy to remember who spilled the blood of his father."

"Why, that's damn touching, ma'am," Keller said.

She nodded. "One day, he'll come looking for you."

Keller pointed at Virgil. "Him?" All three men laughed.

Their laugh echoed through Mary's mind the remainder of her life.

1

El Paso, 1899:
Even the cacti by the ferry landing wilted beneath the afternoon sun. The muddy waters of the Rio Grande slid sluggishly under the bridge linking El Paso with Juarez. A line of wagons and horses bound for Mexico were lined up at the foot of the bridge, blocked for the previous half hour by a broken-axled wagon which had dumped a load of adobe bricks on the roadbed. The heat so sapped the energy of everyone that few even bothered to fan themselves. What good would it do? The sun was so strong and they were so weak.

Slumped forward with his elbows resting on his knees, Virgil Child sat motionless in the seat of his freight wagon, his eyes fixed on the Mexicans trying to repair the axle and pick up the bricks. The hot air scorched his lungs with every breath. He flicked his finger at a fly crawling up the reins resting

15

easily in his hand and ignored the sudden commotion in line behind him.

Virgil was as lean as the desert landscape and as muscled as the mountains to the north. Freighting gave a man muscles and Virgil had been freighting for six years, making daily trips between El Paso and Juarez, loading and unloading his wagon with everything from wagon wheels to flour sacks to coffins. He'd developed a reputation as a dependable freighter and had made decent money. He could've made more by adding wagons, taking on men and expanding his operation, but his mother was in ill health and he had to care for her when she needed him, just as she had cared for him when he was young.

His mother worked and lived in a modest house in the bad section of town. Her neighbors were the denizens of brothels and saloons. Virgil was at the age now where he wondered if his mother had been a prostitute and he her bastard son. He'd never known her to take in men. She did take in laundry, which she washed and ironed for the brothels, and she did take Virgil with her to church every Sunday, but she did not take so much as a glance at any man.

Always his mother had talked about Virgil's father as a prince of a man, as one she

16

loved then and loved even now. She spoke of him so highly that sometimes Virgil wondered if his father was more imagined than real. Had his mother been so ashamed of her past that she made it all up? Virgil would never know. Perhaps it didn't matter; knowing his roots wouldn't put bread on his table, a roof over his head, clothes on his back or boots on his feet.

Behind him the commotion drew closer, a kid shouting for someone. Virgil paid him no mind, just lifted his hat and ran his fingers through his brown hair. From all the time in the sun, his skin was dark enough for him to pass as a Mexican. His blue cotton work shirt was patched in places and his britches were faded from many washings, his mother always insisting on laundering his clothes. If he wasn't the best freighter in El Paso and Juarez, he was certainly the cleanest.

As he tugged his hat back down in place, he heard a Mexican lad call out his name.

Virgil twisted around on his seat, just as a huffing boy of no more than twelve bounded up to the wagon and grabbed the wheel beside Virgil's seat.

"*Señor,* come quick," he gasped. "Your momma, she is going bad, the doctor said. Come quick."

Virgil leaned over the side of the wagon, grabbed the boy by the arm and lifted him up into the wagon seat. Quickly, he released the brake, pulled the reins hard to the left, then slapped them against the rears of his mules. The animals turned sharply away from the bridge as Virgil whistled shrilly.

Gritting his teeth, Virgil steered the wagon through the buggies and pedestrians backed up down the dusty street. Several men cursed his sudden departure. He urged the mules forward and the wagon lurched through the streets of El Paso. The lad at his side grabbed the seat and held on, yelling with glee at the excitement.

Virgil knew his mother was dying from tuberculosis and any moment might be her last. Regardless of who his father had been, she was the one who had raised him and taught him right from wrong.

The wagon careened through the traffic, drawing stares at every house and corner. Virgil turned onto a side street that passed a two-story brothel and led to his mother's house. Out front he saw the doctor's buggy. Virgil bit his lip as he jerked back on the reins and shoved the brake lever with his feet. The wagon vibrated to a stop in front of the modest house and Virgil tossed the reins to the Mexican boy, then jumped off the seat. Hitting the hard pack at a run, Virgil bolted up the two steps, then into the parlor, and turned for his mother's bedroom just as the doctor stopped him at the door.

Rolling the sleeve of his white shirt down, the doctor shook his head.

For an instant, Virgil thought his mother was dead.

"Wish there was more I could do," he said. "She's weak. She may last the night. She may not."

Virgil sighed, then stepped past the doctor into a simple bedroom with a bed, modest bureau, chair and nothing else. Blankets hanging over the windows blocked out the light and any breeze that might slip past the heat. He eased to the bed and stared at his mother. He had always seen her as strong, almost invincible, yet now she seemed so helpless and fragile. Her head was beaded with sweat that matted her gray hair and made her face glisten in the soft light. Virgil took off his hat and began to fan her flushed face.

The gentle wisp of air against her flesh brought a smile to her lips, and her eyes fluttered open. She squinted, then smiled as she recognized Virgil. "I'm weak, son."

Virgil bit his lip, fighting the emotion that was washing over him. As she lifted her feeble fingers, he slid his free hand into hers and sat down beside her on the bed, all the time fanning her.

She began to whisper and Virgil leaned closer to hear her words. "I wish your father'd seen you grow up. You take after him."

He grimaced, thinking she was hallucinating, but he felt her fingers tighten around his. "Who was my father?" Virgil asked, instantly sorry for the question.

Her watery eyes overflowed and tears trailed down her wrinkled cheek. Then she smiled. "Rueben Child was his name. He was a good man, a trusting man." She turned her head and coughed, spewing up a spot of blood on the pillow.

Virgil patted her feeble hand, suddenly cold despite the heat.

"You thought I worked the houses, Virgil, but I never did. No man could ever replace your father."

Virgil felt his throat tightening. "Rest, Momma, please. Rest so you can get better."

Her eyelids dropped, and Virgil would have thought her dead except for the slight rise of her chest as she inhaled.

After a long silence, she spoke. "I'll be better, son, when I see your father across the river. I'm cold now."

Virgil dropped his hat to the floor. How could she be cold when it was so hot in the room? She was drenched with sweat. "I love you, Momma."

The words seemed to give her strength. "Promise me one thing, will you, please?"

"Anything," Virgil replied.

"Bury me beside your father."

Virgil nodded, even though he didn't know much about his father, much less where he was buried. "Where?"

"New Mexico Territory, son, between the Jicarilla and Sacramento Mountains."

Virgil was confused. She had never before talked of those mountains.

She slid her hand from his and pointed to the bureau. "In the top drawer, get the box."

Virgil hesitated.

"Hurry," she said, "hurry."

Virgil stood up and moved to the bureau. He pulled open the drawer and removed a cigar box, then retreated to his mother.

She nodded weakly. "Open it."

By the box's weight, Virgil didn't expect to find anything in it as he lifted the lid, but he was wrong. His eyes focused on a stained handkerchief, neatly folded. He lifted the cloth and noticed a length of lace sewn around but one side. He didn't understand

21

that — or the three splotches of blood and the three names written in his mother's hand on the cloth.

"That's your father's blood and the names of the men who will know where he's buried."

Virgil wondered if she was hallucinating. Virgil mouthed the names on the handkerchief, then looked at his mother. "How'd he die? Was he killed?"

She nodded feebly.

"Why didn't you tell me before?"

"I feared you might take out after his killers, son. I didn't want to lose you. For years I wanted his killers dead, but no more. The church washed away my bitterness, like it washed away my sins. Now, I just want to be buried by your father. He was a good, decent man."

Virgil read aloud the names written in ink upon the cloth. "Ed Keller, Van McCracken and Tom Long. They killed my father?"

"It doesn't matter now, son. The church washed the bitterness from my soul. Don't let it fester in you. Just bury me beside him and leave. He's buried near what must be White Oaks now. He was a decent man, like you. I see much of him in you."

Virgil placed the cigar box atop the bureau, then sat on the bed beside his mother.

22

"I am tired," she said.

He patted her hand.

"I want you to . . ." She sighed. "Just bury me by your father." Her head slowly rolled to one side and her breathing became labored.

She was dying, as sure as Virgil was confused. Why had she waited so long to confide in him? Had she been hallucinating? Virgil knew he would never know for sure.

He waited by her side for more than an hour, her breathing slowing, then strengthening enough for her to say one word.

"Rueben," she called in a strong, almost healthy voice.

After that her breathing became so faint, he failed to realize when it stopped.

2

The gloss of the coffin's varnish reflected a dagger of sunlight as Virgil Child reined up before the cemetery on the outskirts of White Oaks. The rattle of the wagon's chains and the groan of the dry wood fell as silent as the tombstones before him. Virgil stared at the cemetery, then beyond at the mining town scattered across a broad valley between the Jicarilla and Sacramento Mountains. Virgil twisted around in the wagon seat to view the mines that clung like leeches to the mountain to the northwest. Despite the rumble of mine machinery and the smoke from the slender brick stacks of the mine works, Virgil figured the town was past its peak.

He straightened in his seat, set the foot brake and tied the reins of his mule team. Then, he studied White Oaks, wondering if his past was connected to the mining town. A dozen brick buildings stood like monuments up and down the main street. Many lesser structures of wood and adobe were scattered among the brick edifices, like beggars among the wealthy. Beyond the main street and across a narrow creek that cut the town in half stood a two-story brick schoolhouse with a bell tower atop it and children playing outside.

For all the wealth extracted from the stubborn earth beneath White Oaks, only one house showed any pretension of wealth. A two-story red brick house, it sat alone atop a rise on the south side of town. Four chimney tops stood like sentries over its slate roof. The freshly painted wood trim adorned the walls like new medals on a soldier's uniform.

Virgil wondered if he had come on a fool's mission. He had thought about that possibility many times on the six-day ride from El Paso. Until his mother's death, he had never heard of the Jicarillas or Sacramentos, and now here he waited between their broad shoulders. If only the mountains could talk. If only his mother had told him more or told him sooner. Then, he could have at least asked her for the truth about his father.

"Why?" he muttered to his mother's coffin in the wagon bed.

A passing rider bound for White Oaks astride a chestnut gelding stared at the coffin. Virgil scowled at the rider, who nudged his gelding into a canter and rode on. All the way from El Paso, people had stared at him and his cargo. Virgil was tired of their meddling nature, tired of their suspicious glances, tired of the few questions they were bold enough to ask. He begrudged them their curiosity, even though he had so many questions in need of answers himself.

He lifted his hat and ran his fingers through his brown hair, moist with perspiration. After snugging his hat back in place, he wiped his damp fingers on his britches. For a moment his hand came to rest on the butt of his revolver, and then it moved toward his vest pocket. He wormed his finger and thumb into the pocket and extracted the bloodstained handkerchief his mother had revealed to him from her deathbed. Unfolding the handkerchief, Virgil's eyes focused on the three splotches of blood, and then the three names.

"Ed Keller, Van McCracken, Tom Long," he said softly, then yelled the names across the valley. "Ed Keller, Van McCracken, Tom Long."

The rider down the road twisted in his saddle to stare at Virgil, then urged his

26

chestnut into a gallop the rest of the way into town.

"Rueben Child," Virgil said softly as he refolded the cloth and slid it back in his vest pocket.

Virgil stood up, stretched his arms, then stepped on the wagon wheel and jumped to the ground, landing gracefully on his feet. He walked around the wagon, stretching the kinks out of his legs and looking at his meager cargo — his mother's coffin, a shovel and pick, his saddle and gear. He had come prepared to stay a week. If he did not find his father's grave in seven days, he would bury his mother and return to El Paso.

Without directions to his father's grave, Virgil figured the cemetery would be the best place to start, even though he didn't expect to find his father there. That would be too simple. Over the years, he had learned that life was never simple, never prone to give a man the easy way out.

The cemetery was marked by a rectangle of whitewashed rocks lined up around the perimeter, save for a gap to let hearses pass through. The grave markers were a mixture of crude crosses of weathered wood, white-washed stones with names painted across them and fine granite markers etched with

27

the names of the deceased.

Removing his hat, Virgil strode through the gap in the stone border. He saw a movement behind one of the stones, then watched a covey of quail scurry for cover beneath a clump of scrub oak. Slowly, he moved from grave to grave, pausing before each to read the inscriptions, if legible, or to ponder those which had been lost to the ravages of sun, snow and time. Every grave was mounded with stones from the rocky ground. A few graves had no marker, their occupants as anonymous as his own father. Virgil paused before the biggest marker of all, a granite obelisk that stood ten feet tall. Carved in the stone was the name Constance Keller. Virgil wondered if the deceased woman, just over two years dead, was related to Ed Keller. Seeing the name gave him hope he might indeed be able to find his father's grave.

Moving on, Virgil explored the cemetery, grave by grave. For a half hour, Virgil hoped he might find a marker with Rueben Child's name upon it so he could put his mother and his own curiosity to rest. As he had expected, it was not to be. No grave wore at its head a stone or wooden marker with Rueben Child's name upon it. Life was never simple, Virgil thought as he stepped beyond the cemetery's stone boundary and replaced his hat.

Stopping beside his two mules, he checked their harnesses to make sure they hadn't rubbed sores on their shoulders. Satisfied that the animals were okay, he edged toward the wagon until he saw a rider approaching from town. This man, too, was staring, and Virgil glared back, tired of folks showing too much interest in his business. Virgil spat at a stone in front of his team, then watched the rider turn off the main road onto the trail to the cemetery. As the rider neared, Virgil saw the badge pinned to his chest.

He had no cause to fear the law, so he stepped around the team to face his visitor, who nodded as he stopped his bay not fifteen feet from Virgil. The lawman stood up in his stirrups, studying the coffin, then eased back down in the saddle as his gaze fell to Virgil.

"Announce yourself," the lawman said, his voice as steady as his gaze.

Virgil removed his hat. "Virgil Child of El Paso."

"Marshal Nap Webb of White Oaks. You weren't planning on causing any trouble, now were you, Virgil?"

Webb sat easily in the saddle, as patient as ice. He was a small man, not five and a half feet tall by Virgil's estimation, and skinny as a sapling. He had high cheekbones and hawklike eyes that seemed capable of reading a man's thoughts before he'd finished them himself.

"I'm not looking for trouble." Virgil replaced his hat.

"Well, that's good, Virgil, 'cause one of my friends rode into town saying there was a fellow acting crazy as a loon out at the cemetery, making all sorts of noises."

Virgil shrugged. "I was clearing my lungs."

Webb scratched his chin. "Yelling ain't generally a crime, unless it's disturbing the peace, but you're too far from town for that so I can't rightly arrest you, me being a lawman that does things rightly."

Virgil angered at the marshal's intrusion.

"What brings you to White Oaks? We don't get many visitors carrying a coffin. Hope you ain't planning on filling it here."

"I came from El Paso to bury my mother."

Webb looked at the cemetery, then took off his hat. "Sorry to hear that, Virgil. You planning on digging the grave yourself? I'm sure I can find a few men in need of a dollar or two if you want help. Or even the undertaker, though he'll charge more."

Virgil shook his head. "I promised to bury her beside my father, and he's not buried in the cemetery."

"Where's he buried?"

"Don't know. You ever heard of a man named Rueben Child?"

Webb wrinkled his nose and shook his head. "The name don't mean a thing to me, and I've been in these parts for more than ten years now." He pulled a tobacco pouch from his shirt pocket and began to roll himself a cigarette. When he finished making his smoke, he offered the pouch to Virgil.

Waving the tobacco aside, Virgil shrugged. "Momma never said much about him until the night she died. Made me promise to bury her at his side, somewhere between the Jicarillas and the Sacramentos." Virgil pointed to the mountains surrounding White Oaks. "That's them, isn't it?"

Webb nodded. "That's what everybody in these parts calls them. Named for the Jicarilla Apache before they were sent south to the reservation. It's just as well — the Apache wouldn't have known what to do with the gold that prospectors found in the seventies."

Virgil nodded. "That'd likely be the time my father died then, if my momma's right."

"Odd, a woman not telling her son about his father," Webb mused before taking a

31

drag on his cigarette.

How could Virgil answer that? Had his mother been a fallen woman and unwilling to admit the truth to her son? Was there some dark secret his mother wanted to take to her grave? Had she turned to her religion in her later years to make amends for a sordid past? Had Rueben Child ever really existed? Virgil shrugged. "Momma wasn't much of a talker."

Webb exhaled a ribbon of smoke. "Aren't many men left around these parts from those early days in White Oaks — a dozen or less, and not all of them men of decent character."

Virgil stamped his feet and bit his lip.

"You wouldn't be hiding something from me, now would you?"

"Wish I had something to hide."

Webb pulled the cigarette from his lips and pointed it at Virgil. "Folks'll be nosing around about you when they see you come into town with a coffin. I can let the undertaker know so he can keep the body for a few days."

"I'd be obliged."

"Now he'll want a few dollars, you understand?"

Virgil nodded. "I can afford it."

"Tell you what," Webb offered. "I'll ride

on into town, check with the undertaker and meet you at Gus Shinn's saloon."

"Sure thing, Marshal."

Webb reined his horse about and headed for White Oaks. Virgil lingered a few minutes, taking in the mountains studded with juniper, piñon, scrub oak, and cedar. Virgil rechecked the harnesses on his mules, then examined the wagon wheels for split spokes or slipped rims. A man who handled freight knew to take care of his team and his wagon. They were, after all, his livelihood. Finally satisfied the marshal had had enough time to conduct his business, Virgil climbed back into the wagon seat and aimed his team for White Oaks.

He passed the road to the Deadman Mine back to the northwest, then at the edge of town rode by the mine works of the South Homestake Mine. The rumble of machinery gave off a low growl, as if the earth itself were complaining. Once beyond the South Homestake, he aimed his wagon toward the main street. Turning down the street, he began to look on both sides for Gus Shinn's saloon.

As he drove, he realized people were staring at him and his cargo. He was glad when he spotted Shinn's saloon midway down the street. He drew up his wagon outside the

33

double door, set the brake, tied the reins and jumped for the ground. Landing nimbly, he strode inside. It took Virgil's eyes a moment to adjust to the dim light, then he spotted Marshal Nap Webb.

With a wave of his arm, the marshal invited Virgil to the bar.

"Gus serves beer, but no hard liquor," Webb announced. "Henry Reed, he has the biggest mercantile in White Oaks and he's the one that sells liquor, though his ain't no saloon, just a mercantile with a room off the side where men can go in and fill a jigger or a flask with rye or bourbon."

"A beer's fine," Virgil responded.

Webb motioned for the bartender to draw another beer. "The undertaker's square to keep your mother for a dollar a day."

Virgil nodded as the bartender brought him his beer. "That'll be fine."

"I've been thinking how we could help you."

Virgil sipped at the beer, wondering what the marshal could do, especially if Virgil was chasing a ghost.

"Of the dozen men still about that were around back then, I figure your best bet is White Oaks' top citizen. He lives in that big red house on the south side of town, him and his daughter. He was one of the first

34

Virgil nodded absently, lifting his mug and studying the beer as it sloshed around the glass.

"Beer okay?" Webb asked.

Letting out a deep breath, Virgil looked at the marshal. "Been a long ride from El Paso. I just want to bury my mother and get back to Texas."

Webb cocked his head at Virgil, then set his jaw. "Something wrong with New Mexico?"

Virgil looked back at his beer. "Not a thing, just that I got business I need to attend in El Paso."

"What kind of business?"

"Freighting."

"All that toting's bad on your back."

"Not as bad as toting a badge."

Webb jerked his cigarette from his lips and laughed robustly. He slapped the bar and shook his head.

Virgil finished off the beer, then sat the mug down on the bar. He could tell the marshal wanted to spend more time talking, but he was anxious to visit Ed Keller and inquire about his father's grave. "Marshal, thanks for your hospitality, but I best be taking care of my mother and visiting Mr. Keller. Where would I find him?"

The marshal nodded. "Generally at his

home, the brick mansion on the hill, though occasionally at the Deadman Mine he owns."

"Obliged," Virgil said, then wiped his lips with the sleeve of his shirt. He turned and marched outside into the sunlight. He shielded his eyes, then cursed at the half dozen men standing around the wagon, speculating on the coffin. "Get away, you sons of sheep," he growled, bounding off the plank walk and onto the dusty street.

The spectators stepped back as Virgil bounced from a wheel hub into the wagon seat. He quickly untied the lines, released the brake, rattled the reins and whistled. The mules danced forward to the music of jingling trace chains, creaking leather and dry, squeaking wood. "Giddyup," Virgil yelled as he swung the wagon around in the street, coming close to a couple of spectators. They cursed and shook their fists as Virgil retreated down the street.

Virgil glanced between buildings toward the red brick mansion on the hill. He wondered if the secret of his father's death could be found behind those walls. As he rode down the street, he saw Weatherby's Funeral Parlor, a modest building with two open coffins behind a display window. He considered stopping and leaving his mother's coffin, but he was anxious to question Keller. If Keller knew, perhaps Virgil could find his father's grave and bury his mother in time to leave White Oaks the next day.

He steered the wagon around a corner and started up a sloping street that leveled out, then climbed again toward the rise and the Keller house. Virgil studied the brick mansion, with its slate roof and freshly painted trim. A waist-high ornamental iron fence surrounded the house. Virgil wondered what it must be like to have the money for such a fine home and for such a fence, which served no purpose other than displaying the wealth of its owner.

Virgil halted the wagon atop the hill and set the brake lever. He stared a moment at the house, thinking he saw the dark maroon drapes move behind one of the tall double windows. He lowered himself from the wagon, tucked in his shirt, straightened his vest and started for the iron gate. As he lifted the latch, he was certain he saw movement behind the drapes. Somebody knew of his presence. He wondered if his observer was Ed Keller. He shoved the gate open. The hinges screeched and groaned for want of a little grease. Virgil shook his head. Something was wrong with a man who could afford an iron fence, but was too cheap — or inattentive — to grease its hinges.

Virgil strode up the steps to a narrow, covered porch, a porch much too small for such a large house. Virgil had yet to meet Ed Keller, but he didn't think much of him. A man with a small porch wasn't sociable. At the thick mahogany door, Virgil grabbed the lion-head brass knocker and pounded it against its brass plate. He retreated a step and waited for someone to come to the door. He thought he heard footsteps, then a muffled voice, but he could not be certain.

Receiving no response, he grabbed the knocker again and pounded harder and longer, the nearby windows rattling at the impact. Releasing the knocker, he crossed his arms over his chest and retreated a step. He had not come to this house angry, but his disposition was quickly changing. Why should Ed Keller be afraid to answer his door?

Just as Virgil was about to step to the door and knock again, he saw the brass knob turn and the door crack open wide enough for a Mexican woman to show her face.

She forced a nervous smile. *"Si, señor."*

"I'm here to see Ed Keller." He stepped toward the door.

The Mexican woman grimaced. "He's

busy. Does he know you?"

Virgil slipped his boot toward the crack in the door so she could not shut it before he received a satisfactory answer. "Not yet. I just need to ask him some questions. I'll be on my way once I get the answers."

The housekeeper glanced to her side a moment, and Virgil realized her boss was likely standing behind the door, giving her instructions.

"Please, *señor,* go away or he will send for the law."

Virgil nodded, "The law sent me."

The housekeeper looked to her side again.

"Marshal Nap Webb told me to talk to Ed Keller. I'm looking for a grave. The marshal said Mr. Keller was the man who might know."

"No, *señor,* he knows nothing."

"Then just let me talk to him."

"No, I cannot," she replied, then started to close the door, but Virgil's boot prevented her from shutting it.

Her eyes widened with surprise as she pushed against the door.

Virgil stopped the door with his hand, giving it a sharp push. No match for his strength, the housekeeper moved backward, but the door hit more resistance and Virgil knew Ed Keller was behind it.

41

"No, *señor, por favor.* He is busy."

His patience at an end, Virgil patted the gun at his hip. "Tell Mr. Keller I'm wearing a six-gun and it'll put a nice hole in the door if he doesn't let me in for a moment."

The housekeeper fled, the fall of her shoes on the hardwood floor the only sound for a moment.

"I don't keep money in the house," came a man's voice from inside.

"This isn't about money." Virgil shoved the door and it swung full open on its hinges, banging into the wall. In the dimness of the room, Virgil saw a slender man squinting at him until he stepped from the sunlit door. For an awkward moment, the two men stood studying each other, neither saying a word.

The man Virgil assumed was Ed Keller wore a wool suit and a look of hate. His thinning hair with a widow's peak was the dark red of dried blood. He stood blinking his eyes and biting his lip, his gaze moving back and forth between the gun on Virgil's hip and the wagon parked in view of the door.

"Are you Ed Keller?"

The man hesitated before nodding, then stood still as a statue, the movement of his eyes the only sign he was living and breathing.

"I came to ask you some questions, then I'll be leaving." Virgil paused. "If I get answers."

"Nothing I know can be of any help to you, not now, not ever." The voice was filled with venom.

Virgil removed his hat. "I came all the way from El Paso to bury my momma."

"Then bury her and be gone."

"She wanted to be buried beside my father." As he spoke, Virgil saw the Mexican housekeeper poke her head tentatively from what looked to be a parlor adjacent to the entry hall.

Keller noticed her and pointed to a room on the opposite side of the hall. "What we have to discuss, we'll discuss in there."

Virgil nodded and started that way.

Keller snapped his fingers and pointed at the door as he entered. The housekeeper scurried from the parlor to the door and closed it the moment Virgil passed through.

Virgil entered an office with a big rolltop desk, a table covered with surveyor's maps and a wall lined with bookcases overflowing with leather-bound volumes.

Keller marched to his desk, picked up a pen and dipped it in an inkwell. "I'm a man of means in these parts," he announced. "How much will it take for you to bury your mother and leave? A thousand dollars? Two thousand?"

Virgil shook his head. "All it will take is the truth and answers to a few questions."

"Five thousand?"

"No."

"Ten thousand? That's my final offer."

Virgil moved his fist toward his vest pocket and saw Keller's eyes widen as his hand eased past his revolver. Slowly, Virgil pulled the blood-stained handkerchief from his vest.

Keller's sallow flesh paled as Virgil unfolded the cloth.

"You seen this before?"

Keller shook his head. "I don't know what it is."

Virgil knew Keller was lying and scared. "What are you hiding?"

"I don't know what you're talking about."

"It's the blood of my dead father, Keller, and that's not all. Your name, in my momma's hand, is written on the cloth. Where's he buried?"

Keller shook his head and threw the pen on his desk. "Get out," he mumbled, running his hands through his red hair.

Virgil slapped his hat back on his head

and shook the stained cloth at Keller. "You haven't seen the last of me, Keller. I'll keep pestering you until I get an answer." He folded the handkerchief, and as he returned it to his vest, he let his hand pause over his revolver, enjoying the fear in Keller's eyes.

Behind him, Virgil heard a sudden noise, and he spun around at the sound of the door flying open.

"Father," came a voice as soft as silk, "the wagon in front, what does it mean?"

Virgil removed his hat and held it over his heart as a young woman, maybe eighteen at the oldest, burst into the room. She had long red hair and skin as milky as fresh cream. When she realized someone was in the room with her father, her face reddened with embarrassment.

"I'm sorry," she said. "I should have realized you might have a visitor, but the wagon outside frightened me. There's a coffin."

"It's my mother," Virgil explained.

"I'm terribly sorry," she said, her words as sincere as her eyes. "I lost my mother just over two years ago. I wasn't quite sixteen."

Virgil grimaced. "My condolences."

She nodded gently. "I miss her so."

"Prissy," said Keller, "our visitor must be going."

45

"But we haven't been introduced, Father," Priscilla answered. "You're forgetting all the manners Mother taught you."

"I'm Virgil Child," he announced, holding out his hand.

Priscilla slipped her hand in his and shook it gently. "You aren't from these parts."

Virgil looked around from Priscilla to her father. "Don't rightly know, ma'am. Fact is, I may have spent a few years around here when I was too young to remember. My father's supposed to be buried around here, and my mother wanted to rest by his side."

Priscilla lifted her hand from Virgil's. "She must have loved him greatly."

"I never knew him."

"At least I'll always have memories of my mother."

Virgil nodded, then looked at Keller. "Memories, though, aren't always good."

Keller gritted his teeth as Virgil turned back to Priscilla.

"Your father knew my father, ma'am, and I was hoping he could help me find his grave."

"Is that true, Father? You must help him find the grave."

Keller stood glaring at Virgil. "I don't remember him, Prissy, so I can't be much help."

46

Priscilla stepped past Virgil to her father. "You must," she said as she threw her arms around him, "you simply must help him."

4

Ed Keller stood glaring, first at Priscilla, then at Virgil. He slowly shook his head, then scraped his daughter's arms away from his. Priscilla's gaze fell and her eyes clouded at his words. "Don't concern yourself with these matters, Prissy." Keller studied Virgil. "Get out and don't come back."

Virgil replaced his hat and licked his lips. "Your name's on the handkerchief."

"What handkerchief?" asked Priscilla.

"Shut up." Keller slapped her across the cheek.

Tears welled in the young woman's eyes and she lifted her hand to her cheek. "I'm sorry," she said, her head and her voice dropping.

Virgil clenched his jaw, wanting to give Keller a fistful of his own medicine.

Priscilla bit her lip. Virgil wished he could read her mind and learn what was behind the surprise in the emerald green of her eyes. She shook her head and ran out the door. Behind him Virgil heard the clatter of her shoes running up the stairs.

Keller pointed his finger at Virgil's nose. "You shouldn't have come to White Oaks, boy."

"You don't control me or what's right, Keller."

The mine owner wagged his finger at Virgil. "You best dig a hole for your mother, plant her and get out of White Oaks before you find yourself in a hole of your own."

Virgil backed toward the door. "Whatever you're hiding, I expect to find out. Momma didn't say you killed my father, but she didn't say you didn't either."

Keller scowled. "You should've taken the money. It's more than a man like you'll see in a lifetime."

Virgil nodded. "Maybe so, but my conscience is clear. I haven't killed anybody — yet."

Paling visibly, Keller lowered his outstretched finger to hide the tremble of his hand. The threat hung in the air as Virgil backed from the office and escaped out the front door. He bounded down the steps and strode across the graveled path to the gate. Lifting the latch, he shoved open the groaning gate and marched out, not bothering to close it. He pulled himself into his wagon. After untying the reins, he released the brake and whistled at the team of mules.

Glancing over his shoulder as the mules lurched ahead, he saw Keller staring at him through his tall office window. To Virgil's surprise, he observed Priscilla watching him from an upstairs window. He could have sworn she waved at him. He shook the reins, urging the mules on as they started down the slope and away from the Keller place. He didn't know what to think about Ed Keller. As sure as Virgil was in New Mexico Territory, Keller had had a hand in his father's death, but that had been years ago. What was Keller afraid of?

Though Virgil had questions about Keller and Keller's part in his father's death, he had even more about his mother. Why had she waited up until the day of her death to give him a few fragments of his father's history? She had always spoken of his father in vague, general terms, and never about his death until she was on the threshold of her own. She had been so secretive that Virgil, as he grew older and wiser in the ways of men, figured she might, in her youth, have been a fallen woman. She had lived in a bad section of El Paso where many sinful women worked, but Virgil had never seen her with another man. She did hard but honest laundry work by day and read her Bible at night.

Virgil wasn't sure when she'd found religion. He could remember a time when he did not go to church, but there were later memories of his mother dragging him to church every Sunday. She always made Sunday Mass and went in for confession weekly.

She read the Bible a lot and the Scriptures brought her great comfort, though the verse he heard her repeat most often seemed so unnatural coming from his mother's lips. She was gentle and kind, but often he had heard her repeat that vengeance is the Lord's to reap.

Maybe all those years the church had given her a solace that her husband had once provided. If his father was indeed killed by the men listed on the handkerchief, why did he not learn of this as he grew up? Had she hidden the fact to protect Virgil from taking the trail of vengeance? A plant is only as healthy as the soil it grows in. Maybe she didn't want to poison his roots with the bitterness of vengeance. He twisted around and looked at the coffin tied down in back of the wagon. She was so close, yet beyond the reach of his questions. He straightened around and turned the wagon toward the center of White Oaks.

Why had she waited so long to reveal so little about his father? And the handkerchief — why had she given it to him? Why had she only said the men whose names were upon it would know where his father was buried? Did they know because they had killed him? Maybe she had understood his own doubts about her past and had wanted to help remove them. Now, though, he had more questions than doubts.

Virgil shook his head. He could spend a lifetime in White Oaks and never answer them all. He sighed as he guided the team onto the main street and started back toward Weatherby's Funeral Parlor. Reaching the modest wooden building, Virgil halted the team and studied the dingy white-washed walls, which contrasted with the sparkling clean of the display windows that gave pedestrians a chance to view two cloth-lined coffins. As Virgil tied the leather lines, the parlor door swung open and a tiny man in a long-tailed black coat and silk tie emerged. In the middle of the tie was a diamond as phony as his smile.

"I'm Tyrone Weatherby, proprietor of the best funeral parlor in White Oaks."

In no mood for small talk, especially with

several people stopping to stare, Virgil shook his head. "The only funeral parlor, don't you mean?"

"Same difference, wouldn't you say?"

Virgil looked at the spectators, who had gathered in a semicircle not fifteen feet away. "You folks go on about your business and I'll go on about mine." A few hesitated, but Virgil stared hard at them and they began to drift away. Shrugging, he climbed out of the wagon and prepared to introduce himself.

The undertaker beat him to it. "You must be Virgil Child. The marshal told me about you. Not many men tote a coffin around."

"Marshal Webb said you could put up my mother until I find where to bury her."

Weatherby nodded. "A dollar a day, I believe, is what I told the marshal. Five days' payment in advance."

Virgil shoved his hand into his britches pocket and pulled out a leather pouch made from a bull's scrotum. The pouch was stuffed with more than five hundred dollars from his freighting business and from the meager amount of money he found among his mother's things. He pulled out five dollars and shoved the money at the undertaker.

Weatherby snatched the money from Virgil's hand, but his eyes focused on the money pouch. "You can keep her here as long as you like, but one thing." Weatherby paused, pursing his lips.

Virgil cocked his head at Weatherby. "What?"

"Your mother — she was embalmed, wasn't she? If not, I need to do that. It'll be an extra charge, of course."

Virgil nodded. "It was done in El Paso."

The undertaker seemed disappointed that he wouldn't be able to charge Virgil anything else. "You don't know where you want to bury her?" he asked, his smile returning at the thought of an extended search for the proper place.

"I'm looking for the grave of Rueben Child. You know the cemeteries in these parts, don't you, Weatherby? You ever see a grave for a Rueben Child?"

Weatherby shrugged. "Don't recall seeing such a name. When did he die?"

"Some twenty years ago."

Weatherby clucked his tongue. "Weren't many folks here then except Apaches, a few prospectors and even fewer men trying to start ranches. I didn't come to White Oaks until seven years ago."

Virgil turned to the wagon and started

unstrapping the ropes that held the coffin in place.

Weatherby marched over to help. "You see occasional graves that old or older about the countryside, but they either never had a marker or somebody used it for firewood. Who's to say who's buried there."

Virgil tossed an end of rope over the coffin, then moved to loosen the second line securing the wooden box.

"Your coffin, there, looks like one of the ones made across the border in Mexico."

Virgil nodded. "I do a lot of freight business in Mexico. This coffin seemed as good as any."

"Well, it ain't. I've got a better coffin I can sell you, one much more appropriate for your mother."

"She won't know the difference."

"You will," replied Weatherby.

Instead of removing the final rope, Virgil started snugging the coffin back down. "Give me my five dollars back," he said over his shoulder.

Weatherby grimaced, then stuttered. "But, but, but. . . ."

Dropping the rope, Virgil turned around. "If you want the money that comes from keeping her, then shut up. Do you want it or not?"

Weatherby nodded vigorously, uncertain for a moment if he should answer aloud. "Okay, okay."

Virgil turned around and began to loosen the rope again.

"Let me help untie it," offered Weatherby.

"Too late," Virgil shot back, brushing Weatherby aside so he could go to the end of the wagon and drop the tailgate. He crawled into the wagon bed and grabbed the coffin by the handles on each side. Then, he pulled the coffin to the end of the wagon.

"We need to get someone else to help carry her inside?" Weatherby asked.

Virgil shook his head. "She was a frail woman when she died." He jumped from the wagon to the ground and grabbed a pair of handles on the near side of the coffin.

Weatherby looked at the five dollars in his hand, then at Virgil. The undertaker shoved the money in his pocket, jumped beside the coffin and grabbed the handles. "I'm ready."

Together, Virgil and the undertaker removed the coffin from the wagon and toted it inside the funeral parlor, which had the musty aroma of dried flowers and stale chemicals. The undertaker directed Virgil past a viewing room and into a storeroom where coffins were stacked against the wall.

Weatherby nodded toward a pair of saw-horses. "That's where we'll put her."

Virgil was surprised by the frail undertaker's strength. He easily hoisted the coffin high enough to rest on the sawhorses, then let it down softly.

"Anything else I can do for you, Virgil?"

Scratching his chin, Virgil studied the undertaker. "You can see that I get two tombstones of fine granite. One to read 'Rueben Child, husband of Mary,' and the other to say 'Mary Child, wife of Rueben.' "

"What about the dates?"

Virgil shrugged. "I don't know all the dates, and they don't matter."

"Yes, sir," Weatherby replied.

"Another thing. You have any names of folks that might have been around back then I could ask about my father's grave?"

Weatherby nodded. "Ed Keller was one of the first. He's likely the best."

"I saw Keller before coming here. He's no help."

The undertaker shook his head. "Too bad, he's the best possibility. There were a couple others here about the same time, I suppose. Van McCracken and Tom Long are both about."

His eyes narrowing, Virgil looked at Weatherby. "What about them?"

Weatherby kneaded his hands together. "Van McCracken and Tom Long were once Keller's partners, but Keller bought them out. Long and McCracken swore they were both cheated out of their shares of Deadman Mine and the Keller Gulch claim. They're both still around these parts, though I don't know why. McCracken's nothing but a drunk who hangs around town and begs for drinks. Long's a gambler, a tough and dangerous man who seems to live pretty well off his winnings or his mischief. Besides McCracken and Long, there's maybe three or four cowmen who might have been in the area back then."

Virgil nodded. "Thanks. Where's the best place to room?"

"Try the Hotel Ozanne, a block west and a block south of here."

"Obliged. I'll be by to see you and pay you another five days if I'm in town longer."

Virgil retraced his steps out of the storeroom and past the viewing room. When he stepped outside, he found Marshal Nap Webb waiting by the wagon.

"Child, we need to talk."

Virgil studied Webb. This was the look he had seen at the cemetery when Webb was suspicious of his presence, not the friendly look he had seen in the saloon. "About what, Marshal?"

"About your threat to kill Ed Keller and his daughter."

what, Marshal?"

"About your threat to kill Ed Keller and his daughter."

5

Virgil felt his lips tighten in anger. He wadded his fists and stepped toward the wagon, shaking his head.

Marshal Nap Webb took a drag on his cigarette, then flung it into the street as Virgil moved toward him. His hand dropped to his waist and near the Colt .45 which rested on his hip.

"I didn't threaten Keller or his daughter, Marshal."

"That's not how Mr. Keller tells it. He said you threatened to shoot him unless he let you in and then you slapped Priscilla. I seen her face and there's a welt across her cheek."

"Keller slapped her."

Webb shook his head. "That's not what Mr. Keller said."

"Keller's a liar."

"The girl said it, too."

Virgil swallowed hard, more disappointed

than angered that Priscilla had lied as well.

"Mr. Keller said you came to kill him and the girl."

"Hell, Marshal, I didn't even know he existed until you pointed me to his house."

"Did you pull a gun on him or the girl?"

"Hell no, Marshal. I told him I was armed and planned to put a bullet in his door if he didn't let me in."

"Keller said you're carrying a list of people you plan to kill, something on a bloody handkerchief. That true?"

Virgil spat toward the wagon and squeezed his fists even tighter.

"You carrying a list or a bloody handkerchief, Child?"

"It's no matter, Marshal."

"It is if it's got Keller's name on it. Let me see it."

Nodding, Virgil started for his vest pocket, but his hand froze as Webb put his hand on the butt of his own revolver. "It's in my vest pocket," Virgil explained.

His hand resting on his revolver, Webb nodded. "Go ahead."

Virgil gradually slid his hand into his vest and pulled out the cloth that was such a mysterious part of his mother's legacy. Before he extracted the handkerchief, he looked around, seething at the crowd that had gathered to watch. Several were nodding and pointing at him, whispering that he was the one who had come into town with a coffin in his wagon. As he slipped the handkerchief out, he felt as if he was violating his mother's privacy. His hand hung, like the knot in his throat, for a moment, then he stepped to the marshal and offered him the cloth.

Webb took the handkerchief and shook the folds from it. Virgil watched him lift the cloth by the lace on one end. The marshal glanced at the bloodied splotches, then read the names to himself, his lips mouthing the words. Webb looked up at Virgil. "What's the blood?"

"Momma said it was my father's blood."

"And the names?"

Virgil hesitated.

"What do the names mean?"

Virgil stared at the marshal. "Momma said they knew where my father was buried."

"You sure this list ain't why you're here? You came to kill these three men, didn't you?"

"I came to bury Momma beside the father I never knew. When that's done, I'll be leaving White Oaks for a friendlier town. If I came to kill, I wouldn't be hauling a coffin and attracting more attention than a circus wagon."

Webb pursed his lips, then began to refold the handkerchief. He handed it back to Virgil.

"I'll accept your word for it this time, Child, but if there's any trouble, you're the first one I'm coming after."

Virgil slipped the handkerchief back in his vest. "That all, Marshal?"

"For now," Webb replied, backing away from Virgil toward the covered walk in front of Weatherby's Funeral Parlor. "You just remember to keep away from Keller."

Virgil strode to the wagon, climbed into the seat, grabbed the reins and released the brake. He shook the leather reins and the mules danced ahead down the street.

"Welcome to White Oaks," he heard the marshal call in his wake.

He turned south off the main street, then headed west on the next street to find the hotel. His eyes focused on a two-story brick building. He spotted a wooden sign by the door identifying the structure as the Hotel Ozanne. He stopped, set his team and jumped out of the wagon, still simmering from the lies Keller had told about him. He marched up the hotel steps and pushed open the door, causing the bell attached at the top to jingle. A registration desk near the door faced across a small lobby that was furnished with a couple sofas, a half dozen chairs, a pair of tables with lamps and a potbellied stove. The registration counter was vacant and the room was empty except for an aproned man cleaning the windowsills with a feather duster.

The man tossed the feather duster on the nearest chair. "Good afternoon," he said. "Need a room?"

"Could use one. That's why I stopped."

"Some folks stop for information on the stage, since this is the stop in White Oaks," the clerk replied, stepping behind the counter. "How long will you be staying?"

"No longer than I have to."

The clerk, an older man with thinning brown hair and sympathetic eyes, shrugged. "Sorry you haven't found White Oaks to your liking."

"It's not the town, it's the people."

"Hope I'm not one of them that's got your goat. I'm Herb Ozanne, hotel proprietor and manager of the stage line between here, Lincoln and Roswell." He didn't ask Virgil's name, just turned the guest register around and pushed an inkwell and pen toward him.

Virgil grinned at Ozanne. "It's Ed Keller and Marshal Nap Webb."

Ozanne nodded. "Those two are big men

64

in their own minds. Keller's got the wallet and Webb's got the badge. Of the two, Webb's the better man, just that he does too much of what Keller tells him without giving it a second thought."

Virgil dipped the pen in the inkwell and signed the register.

Ozanne turned the book around and looked at it. "Virgil Child, welcome to Hotel Ozanne. You're the one that brought the coffin into town, aren't you?"

Virgil nodded.

Ozanne took in a deep breath, then exhaled slowly. "You're not planning on keeping it here . . . I mean the body . . . ?"

Virgil shook his head. "I've made arrangements for Tyrone Weatherby to hold the coffin. Now, how much do I owe you?"

The proprietor smiled. "You can pay me when you leave."

Virgil cocked his head. "Weatherby made me pay in advance."

Ozanne snickered. "Yeah, but he only gets a customer once. I hope to have him several times." He shoved a key across the counter. "Room number seven. We serve supper from an hour before dark until an hour after dark." He pointed to the door at the back of the entry parlor. "That's the dining room

65

beside the stairway. Anything else you need?"

"A place to stable and feed my team."

"Mayer's livery is a block north on White Oaks Avenue. That's the main street through town."

"Obliged," Virgil said, grabbing the key from the counter and heading back outside to the wagon. He took his bedroll and tow sack of belongings from the wagon and retreated back inside the hotel, striding past Ozanne, who had resumed his feather-dusting. Virgil bounded up the stairs, and found himself in the middle of a long hallway dimly lit by the afternoon's dying sunlight. He spotted number seven, unlocked the door and carried his belongings inside, tossing them on the bed.

He retreated out the door and locked it, then headed back downstairs and out to his wagon, which he drove to the livery stable and paid for five days' care for his mules. He walked back to the hotel, drawing the stares of several men.

At the hotel, he returned to his room and collapsed on the bed beside the tow sack and bedroll. He rolled over on his back, staring at the tin ceiling and wondering why Ed Keller had denied ever knowing his father. He had come to White Oaks to bury his mother, not to murder anyone. But what were they hiding that made them so suspicious of his presence?

He pondered the question and dozed off to sleep. When he awoke, the room was shrouded in the gray light of dusk. He went downstairs to the dining room. Four of the eight tables were filled. Herb Ozanne pointed him to one in the corner and was shortly beside him, filling a cup of coffee and suggesting the beefsteak and creamed potatoes. In a few minutes, Ozanne returned with a heaping plate of victuals, a basket of fresh biscuits and a refill of coffee. When Virgil finished, Ozanne brought him a slice of apple pie. "You didn't order it, but if you don't eat it or don't like it when you're done, it's on the house." Virgil ate it and enjoyed it, then lingered a bit over a final mug of coffee before paying for his supper and stepping outside into the gathering darkness.

His nap had refreshed him enough that he didn't care to retire to his room just yet. Instead, he walked over to the main street to kill time and maybe buy a drink. At the saloon where he had met Marshal Webb earlier, he turned inside and marched up to the counter. The bartender recognized him and nodded.

"Drink's on the house, if you'll tell me who all's listed on the bloody handkerchief."

"It don't matter," Virgil replied.

"It does if they're my customers." The bartender laughed. "What can I get you?"

"A shot of whiskey."

"Wish I could."

"Huh?"

"Beer or wine. That's it."

"No whiskey? Why?"

"No profit in it, not with Henry Reed in town. He runs Reed's Mercantile. He has a room off the side of his store and keeps a couple barrels of rye and bourbon in there. He sells it cheaper than anyone else can afford to and he lets men buy on credit. Most of all, though, wives don't get suspicious when they see their husbands going into the mercantile instead of a saloon."

Virgil stepped away from the bar.

"Sure I can't get you a beer?"

Virgil shook his head. "Tonight, I need something a little stronger." He retreated out the saloon and walked down the street, looking for Reed's Mercantile. Though most of the buildings were dark, a few havens for male entertainment, like the Little Casino Saloon, were lit. The building that shined the brightest, though, was the mercantile on the next block. Virgil ambled toward the

68

store and reached the door just as the clerk was about to twist the Open sign around and close up.

He unlatched the door and stuck his head out. "What you need?"

"A little whiskey."

"We're about to close, but come on in and we'll see to your thirst." The clerk pulled the door open.

Virgil walked in as the clerk shut the door and turned the sign around.

"Liquor's through that door," the clerk pointed. "There's jiggers or you can fill a flask."

Virgil moved between tables of goods toward the door, but stopped just outside when he spotted movement in the room. Virgil saw a table with two whiskey barrels atop it and a skinny man with a sunken chest and sunken eyes. The man seemed to be looking to see if he was being observed. Virgil did not know how the fellow could have missed seeing him, but apparently he did. The fellow squatted down on the floor beneath one of the barrels, opened his mouth beneath the spigot, then turned the handle and gulped down the liquor with abandon.

Virgil cleared his throat and the man twisted the spigot handle and jumped to his feet. He staggered a moment as he seemed to focus his eyes on something far away. Virgil shook his head and entered, spotting clean jiggers, glasses and flasks on a shelf by the door.

He grabbed a flask, then nodded at the skinny fellow, who seemed to be staring intently at him. As he moved to a barrel marked Bourbon, he put the flask under the spigot and began to fill it. The skinny man tiptoed toward him. Virgil watched the old fellow out of the corner of his eye, certain the drunk was going to ask for a drink.

As soon as the flask brimmed with the dark liquid, Virgil turned toward the drunk.

The drunk's red, watery eyes went wide and his mouth gaped open. "Oh, no, no," he said, grabbing his head with his hands.

"What is it?" Virgil asked.

"You know what it is. Don't hurt me," he pleaded, lowering his hands from his head to his chest, where he held his palms together like he was praying.

"I'm not going to hurt you."

The drunk began to tremble.

Virgil reached out to touch him, but the skinny man backed away until he cowered against the wall.

"I'm not going to hurt you," Virgil repeated.

"I knew you'd come back, I knew it." The drunk began to sob in his hands. "I didn't mean to, please don't kill me."

"I'm not going to kill you."

"If I'd killed you, you wouldn't be back. I thought I did. I didn't mean to kill you, but I must not've if you're here with me."

The drunk was becoming more and more incoherent.

Virgil reached for him again; but before he could grab his arm to ease his terror, the drunk darted past him for the door.

The man stumbled out of the side room and ran into a table of leather goods. He bounced away and aimed for the front door. "He's come back to kill me, to kill us all. No, no, please don't."

The clerk darted to unlock the front door before the drunk ran through its glass panes. The clerk won the race and opened the door.

"Out of my way. He's going to kill me."

No sooner had the clerk jerked open the door than the drunk flew outside, screaming for mercy and for help.

Virgil shook his head at the spectacle and shrugged when the clerk turned around. "I didn't touch him. I don't know what got into him, other than some liquor. He was drinking straight from the spigot."

The clerk grinned. "He closes me down every night. Been doing so for years. He's not always that crazy, but there are nights when he's as crazy a man as you'll ever want to see."

Virgil held up the flask. "Makes a man want to give up drinking, doesn't it?"

"Except for every now and then, it sure does. Old Van's the type that drives the Temperance Union women crazier than a wagonload of whiskey. There's enough alcohol in him to pickle half of New Mexico Territory."

Virgil just shook his head.

"Thing I don't understand abut Old Van is why Ed Keller pays for all his alcohol."

"What? Keller covers his liquor?"

"Sure, Keller can afford it."

Then it clicked in his mind. *Old Van!* "Who'd you say that was?"

"Old Van," the clerk repeated.

Virgil lifted the flask to his lips and took a swig on it, then asked another question. "Van who?"

"Van McCracken," the clerk replied. "He was one of the original prospectors in these parts."

Virgil could only shake his head. Van Mc-Cracken's name was also on the blood-stained handkerchief.

72

6

Priscilla Keller glanced shamefully up from the plush sofa where she sat in the finest home in White Oaks. "Why'd you make me lie to the marshal? Virgil Child didn't strike me, you did!"

Anger coursed through his body. Ed Keller would not take impertinence from his daughter. "You do what I say, Prissy."

"You know I don't like you to call me Prissy. Mother named me Priscilla, not Prissy. She'd never order me to lie. It's not right."

Keller stormed to the sofa and jerked his daughter up by the arm. "That boy's out to destroy me, ruin my fortune."

"How can you say that? He's looking for his father's grave so he can bury his mother. It's a decent thing he's doing. I know how he must feel, losing his mother." Her eyes began to well with tears.

Keller released her arm. "I gave your

mother the finest funeral any woman ever had or ever will have in White Oaks."

"She didn't know. You could've done more for her while she was alive."

"Prissy" — he fairly spit the word as he shook his finger at her nose — "don't be questioning me or what I tell you to do again."

"I'm not a baby anymore."

"But you're not a man, neither, and don't you forget that."

She began to sob.

Keller hated that, women crying when things were tough. He would have died years ago if he had been as weak as that. No, he was strong. His strength had made him the richest man in White Oaks. His Deadman Mine was still producing profitable ore, and prospects were still looking good until Virgil Child had knocked on his door.

Keller knew the moment he saw Virgil getting out of the wagon that he was Rueben Child's son. The son bore an uncanny resemblance to the father. All these years he had doubted the boy would ever return to carry out his mother's threat. Even so, he had never forgotten that threat. It had been a nagging worry that had never gone away. It wasn't bad the first ten years after he had killed Rueben Child, because the boy would have still been just that — a boy. But now he was a man, and he had the look of a dangerous one.

Keller cursed himself. He was strong, but when he should've been the strongest and killed the woman and her boy, he had wavered, not wanting to go along with Tom Long's wish to murder them. That was the biggest mistake Keller ever made. But, it was a mistake easily corrected. He had influence, he had power and he had money. He could hire someone to take care of Virgil Child.

Maybe he could get it done without it costing him anything more than the liquor he was already buying. He needed to get out of the house. He was tired of hearing Prissy's sobbing.

He strode out of the parlor and into his office. At his rolltop desk he bent and tugged open the lower drawer. He pulled out a leather shoulder harness which he slid over his arm and shoulders. A man of his prominence should not be seen walking about town with a gun strapped to his waist, but neither should a man of his wealth be unarmed, not with robbers a possibility. From a desk pigeonhole he took out a .38-caliber pistol, then slipped it into the holster.

He stepped to the end of the desk and looked over his shoulder to make sure Prissy wasn't watching. He moved to the wall, then slipped his hand between the wall and the back of the desk to remove a sawed-off shotgun with a shortened stock. Keller broke open the weapon to check its load. The twin chambers each held a shell. Keller snapped the weapon shut and grabbed the leather loop attached to the stock. By slipping the loop over his shoulder, Keller could hide the shotgun beneath his coat. Keller slid the thong over his shoulder, then let the shotgun hang at his side as he walked across the room and lifted his coat.

He slid the coat carefully over his shoulders, adjusted it, then checked to see how far the barrel peeked from the coat. About four inches were visible, but it wouldn't be too obvious, not with it dark outside. Keller knew if he avoided the light of houses or saloons, no one would notice.

Grabbing his hat from the brass hat rack, Keller slipped toward the door. As he stepped onto the hardwood floor of the entryway, he heard Prissy calling him.

"Where are you going?"

It was none of her business. He opened the door and slammed it behind him. The sound of her sobs followed him all the way

76

to the street. He opened his squeaking gate, then melded into the early-evening darkness as quickly as he could.

Van McCracken lived on the opposite side of White Oaks, about as far removed as he could be physically and economically from Keller. McCracken had been there that day when Rueben Child was murdered. He had fired like Long and Keller. With his bullet, he had earned a third of what became known as the Deadman claim. It was Van McCracken who had first found the gold in the placer gravel along what was now known as Keller Gulch. McCracken had even found the vein outcroppings three weeks later. McCracken had celebrated with a bottle of whiskey, and Keller knew he would be able to take over McCracken's third of the claim when the time was right. When that day came and McCracken was drunker than a shipload of sailors, Keller had put a contract under his nose. McCracken had signed away his rights to the claim in exchange for "considerations to be determined." When McCracken sobered up and realized what he had done, he went on a ragged drunk, and some now said he had never sobered up. Keller's "considerations" had been an open account at Reed's Mercantile for all the liquor McCracken could hold.

The night was hot and still, the acrid smell of mining in the air as Keller marched across town. Once he gave the shotgun to McCracken, Keller would tell him to get more shells. That would help provide Keller an alibi in case Marshal Nap Webb took it upon himself to investigate the murder of Virgil Child. The marshal, though, knew when to back off, so Keller figured his only problem was persuading McCracken to kill Child.

Just over a half hour after leaving his squeaking gate at the mansion, Keller eased up to the one-room shack that McCracken called home. The place was unlit and dark, which meant McCracken was either away or passed out on the floor. Keller glanced back toward town and saw the lights being dimmed at Reed's Mercantile. He nodded to himself. McCracken had probably filled a flask before the place closed, then started his trip home.

"Van," Keller called as he stepped up to the front door.

Receiving no answer, Keller kicked open the door and went inside. He heard a scream, then a snarl, and caught his breath as a frightened cat ran by his legs. The room smelled like the cat hadn't been let out in a week. Keller spat on the floor, then dug into his coat pocket for a match, which he flared to life off the tip of his thumbnail.

The sight of McCracken's bed and the dirty, stained sheets almost made him gag. In the near corner he saw a table with a lamp and in the far corner a cheap rawhide chair. He kicked a couple of empty cans out of the way as he stepped to the chair. He sat down, just as the match burnt to the tip of his fingers. He tossed it on the bed and watched it flare out, then glow for a moment on the dirty covers before surrendering to the darkness.

He sat in the darkness, waiting and listening to the sounds of mice scratching on the floor, scrounging for the crumbs from McCracken's meals this week and last. Keller waited thirty minutes or longer before he heard someone approaching. By the irregular footfall, he knew it had to be McCracken. He heard McCracken say a few things that didn't make sense. What else should he expect from a drunk?

McCracken never paused at the open door, never realized that it should have been shut as he had left it. He stumbled in and aimed for the table, fumbling for something until a match came to life between his fingers. He struggled to light a coal-oil lamp with no globe. Slowly a jaundiced light seeped across the room and McCracken turned around, then jumped at the sight of Keller sitting there.

"Damnation, Ed," he cried out, "I'm glad you're here. We've got problems."

Keller shrugged. "Nothing we can't handle. Now what's your problem? Not getting enough liquor?"

"Oh, no, not that. I saw him in the store this evening."

"Who?"

"The man we killed for the mining claim, somebody named . . . what was it? . . . Rube Kid?"

"Rueben Child," Keller corrected, smiling that the uncanny resemblance between the dead father and his living son had confused the drunk.

"We buried him, didn't we, Ed?"

"His wife buried him, Van, yes, sir."

"He looked okay for a man that's been buried that long," McCracken said, stumbling toward his bed and falling atop it.

"Van, I figure he may kill us unless we get him first."

"I don't know, Ed, I don't think he recognized me. Maybe we should just let him be."

Keller shook his head. "He'll just get us

one at a time when we're not looking. You need to shoot him, Van."

Van held his hand up in the air. It trembled like a leaf in the breeze. "My aim's not as steady as it was the first time I killed him."

Keller grinned. "Mine neither. That's why I carry my scattergun with me. You don't need a steady hand with it."

McCracken laughed crazily. "Bet he don't like it that we called it Deadman Mine."

"I'll give you my scattergun, Van, but you need to get him quick, before he gets you."

"You sure a scattergun'll kill him? Our pistols didn't."

"Can't miss, Van."

"I don't know, Ed."

"If you don't, Van, I may tell Old Man Reed to cut off your liquor at the mercantile."

McCracken sat up in bed. "You wouldn't do that, would you, Ed?"

"I wouldn't, but if the fellow got me first, no one would pay for your liquor anymore, Van."

McCracken shook his head, then buried his face in his palms. "You know I've got to have my liquor."

"I know, Van, I know." Keller stood up and slipped his arm out of his coat sleeve, then slid the leather thong from over his shoulder and removed his shotgun. He tossed it on the bed beside McCracken, then put his coat back on.

"All you need, Van, is to buy you some extra shotgun shells, then ambush him some night."

"Thank you, Ed, thank you."

Keller stood up. "I need to get back."

McCracken nodded. "You wouldn't happen to have some liquor on you, would you, Ed?"

7

After a fitful night's sleep, Virgil Child stretched and yawned as he marched down the hotel stairs and prepared to go into the dining room for breakfast. It had been a tiring ride from El Paso, and the events of the previous day had filled him with doubts. This journey had started as a simple task of finding his father's grave. If Ed Keller had just pointed it out to him, he would have buried his mother and gone on, but the longer Keller tried to hide it, the more determined Virgil Child became to find it.

And his chance encounter with Van Mc-Cracken at the mercantile last night raised more questions. He had never seen Mc-Cracken before, but the drunk sure thought he had seen Virgil previously. Was there that much of a resemblance to his father? Virgil knew he would never be able to answer that question.

As he reached the bottom step, he yawned

and rubbed his eyes. When he lowered his hands, he glimpsed a young woman arising from one of the stuffed chairs in front of the registration desk. He recognized Priscilla Keller and gritted his teeth, angered that she had told the marshal he had slapped her. He wondered who she had come to see. It surely couldn't be him. As Virgil turned toward the dining room, she called his name.

"Virgil Child."

Virgil froze, uncertain whether to continue into the dining room or give her a moment. What could she want with him, especially after the accusations she had made? Warily, he turned to face her.

She advanced tentatively, looking over her shoulder for fear that someone might be watching. "I needed to talk to you."

Virgil held up his arm. "Don't get too close or I might slap you again."

"That's what I came to talk to you about." She looked nervously about the room. "Can we visit?" Her voice quivered as she spoke.

Uncertain what to do, Virgil hesitated.

"Please," she pleaded.

Nodding, Virgil motioned her toward the dining room. "I'll buy you breakfast."

Priscilla glanced over her shoulder, then marched by Virgil into the dining room,

84

which was empty except for a single boarder and Herb Ozanne, who recognized Priscilla.

"Good morning, Miss Keller," he announced. "I'm glad you'll be joining us for breakfast."

Priscilla nodded with a slight grimace, then walked past the table where Ozanne had pulled out a chair for her. She headed instead for a corner table out of the line of sight of the door. "This will be better," she said.

"Certainly," replied Ozanne, pulling out a second chair for her.

Virgil trailed behind Priscilla, admiring the cut of her figure, the sway of her hips and the bounce of her red hair. Despite her lie against him, she seemed as innocent as her flawless complexion. He sat down opposite her and faced the door.

Ozanne stood over their table. "What can I get you?"

"Bacon and eggs for me, along with plenty of coffee," Virgil said, "and whatever the lady would like."

Priscilla's pale skin blushed for a moment. "A glass of milk and two biscuits."

Ozanne nodded and walked away.

For a moment, Virgil and Priscilla stared awkwardly at each other, each waiting for the other to say something. As Virgil stared at her, he saw the pink tint across her cheek where her father had slapped her the day before.

"I'm sorry," she said, "for lying to the marshal, but father made me do it. He's scared of you and doesn't like you."

"Do you like me?"

Priscilla smiled tentatively. "I've no reason to dislike you, especially after what you're doing."

"What? Buying you breakfast?"

Priscilla giggled and brushed back a curl of hair that had fallen across her forehead. "Not that, but what you're doing for your mother. That's the nicest thing I ever heard." Her cheeks flushed.

Virgil nodded. "She took in laundry and worked herself to death taking care of me when I was younger. It was the least I could do."

"What about your father?"

Virgil shrugged. "I don't remember him at all. Best I can figure, he was murdered."

"I'm sorry."

"On her deathbed, Momma told me he was buried between the Jicarillas and the Sacramentos. She gave me the names of three men who knew of his grave site."

"Is my father's name on that list?"

Virgil hesitated.

"Is it?" she asked, her voice rising.

Virgil delayed answering the question as Ozanne reached the table with a glass of milk and a pot of coffee.

Ozanne placed the glass in front of Priscilla, then sat the coffeepot down in front of Virgil. "Your breakfast will be out in a few minutes," he said as he turned for the kitchen.

"Was my father's name on the list?"

Virgil nodded.

"What about Van McCracken and Tom Long?"

Virgil knew he couldn't hide the surprise in his face. "Them too."

Priscilla shook her head, then buried her face in her palms. When she looked up, her face was distorted with shame. "There's been stories over the years that my father and his early partners killed a man for his claim. They almost seemed proud of it, naming the claim Deadman Mine."

Virgil shrugged. "There's no proof now, just idle gossip."

"Did you come back to kill them?"

Virgil stared hard into Priscilla's green eyes. They seemed soft and vulnerable, but was this all a trick, just to win his confidence so she could go back and tell her father? Had Keller ordered her to do this, like he had probably ordered her to lie to the marshal? He studied her for a moment, expecting a sign of guile but seeing none.

"I came back to bury my momma. I'll return to El Paso when that's done."

"Even if they did kill your father."

Virgil sighed. "I think Momma never talked about my father's death because she didn't want me growing up with hatred in my heart. It can destroy you. She was a religious woman and used to say that vengeance is the Lord's, not ours."

Ozanne came out of the kitchen with a couple plates and aimed for Virgil's table. He placed a generous serving of bacon, eggs and biscuits before Virgil, then two biscuits on a saucer before Priscilla.

As Ozanne walked away, Priscilla toyed with her biscuits, then broke each in half. "I miss my mother. I never knew how important she was to me until she was gone. My father is a hard man, and she was a gentle woman who was able to soften him around the edges. Without her, the hard edges are coming back. He's hard to live with now."

Virgil shook his head. "If he'd shown me my father's grave, I'da buried my momma and left. You can't change the past, and I'm not even sure I know what the past was for my parents."

Priscilla nibbled at her biscuit, then shook her head. "I don't know what happened. Father was a hard man before he met my mother. She made him respectable. He provided for us well and gave my mother the fanciest funeral White Oaks had ever seen."

"My momma won't have a fancy funeral, just me. No one else knows her or cares."

"*I* do," said Priscilla shyly. "I'll be there, if you let me know."

Virgil smiled. "Thank you."

Priscilla pushed her saucer away, having nibbled no more than half a biscuit. She took her glass of milk and drank it slowly, her eyes focusing on his. When she lowered the glass, Virgil grinned at the white mustache on her upper lip. She patted it away with her napkin.

"I must go," she said as she lowered the napkin, "because my father would not be pleased to learn I've been with you this morning, especially in a hotel, but let me tell you something. There is a man in Carrizozo who might be able to help you, tell you about your father. His name is Jack Parmaley. He was one of the first to settle in these parts and take up ranching. He might know of your father. Mr. Parmaley sold his holdings about five years ago and has enough money that he can stand up to the truth, and my father, if he has to."

"Thank you."

Priscilla dropped her napkin, then reached across the table, her hand outstretched for his. When Virgil placed his fingers in her palm, she squeezed them. "Good luck."

As she released his hand, he arose from his chair and moved to help her up from hers. "Perhaps I can see you again."

"I would like that, but you must not come to my house. My father would never allow you inside. I will get a message to you." She stood and smiled at him. "Good-bye."

Virgil watched her disappear out the door. He hoped her father did not learn of her visit, because Virgil had seen Ed Keller's anger explode upon Priscilla and he did not care for that to happen again. He sat back down and finished his breakfast.

Ozanne wandered over to check on Virgil. "Need jelly for your biscuits?"

"I've had plenty," he answered. "I just want to have a couple more cups of coffee."

"She's a pretty young lady, isn't she?"

Virgil nodded.

"She seems too delicate to be Ed Keller's offspring. Now, her mother was as kind a woman as ever lived. A lot of folks never understood their marriage."

"Money?"

Ozanne shook his head. "Those that didn't know Connie Keller might say that, but those who knew her knew she didn't have a greedy bone in her body. I guess she saw more in Ed Keller than anybody else ever did. Or maybe, she was able to draw the best out of him. Nobody'll say much about Ed Keller because he has so much money, but not many folks care for him in these parts."

Virgil studied his coffee cup and shook his head.

"And he won't like you seeing his daughter. No, sir, he's tried to shelter her from fellows. One local took to courting her a year ago, and I'll be damned if Keller didn't pay him a thousand dollars to leave Priscilla and White Oaks. Money's bought Keller just about everything he's wanted in life, except happiness." Ozanne laughed. "Didn't mean to make a darn speech."

Virgil nodded.

At the sound of a couple of customers entering the dining room, Ozanne turned away and moved to seat them at a table. Virgil finished his coffee, dug out his money pouch and left more than enough on the table to cover the meal.

He returned upstairs to his room, buckled

on his gun belt and grabbed his hat as he left. He locked the door and bolted down the stairs and out of the hotel. White Oaks was shaded by the mountains to the east, so it was pleasant now, but once the sun cleared the mountains, it would be another scorching day. Virgil marched over to the main street and the stables where he had left his team and wagon. He saddled up one of his mules and rode out of town past the cemetery just as the sun began to peek over the mountains behind him.

To the north, he saw the various mine works scattered over the mountainside, their tall stacks glowing in the early-morning sunlight. The largest of the mine works belonged to the Deadman Mine, Keller's firm. Virgil studied the Deadman claim, which stretched from the base of the mountain down the ravine called Keller Gulch. Though he couldn't put his finger on it, there was something haunting about the gulch, something that seemed to uncover distant memories buried somewhere within his mind.

He drew up his mule and studied the mountainside, then looked down the gulch. Had he ever lived there with his mother and his father? He was touched by a tinge of guilt that he had ever doubted his mother's occasional veiled stories about his father. He shook his head, then nudged his mule toward Carrizozo, twelve miles distant, and Jack Parmaley.

Though Virgil had covered the same road on the way in to White Oaks from El Paso, he was always amazed at how different country looked from a different direction. He didn't push the mule, but took in the land, wondering if some of it might have been his had his father lived, contemplating what it would be like to be rich had his land had gold upon it and regretting that his mother had had to work herself to death to support him as a kid. By the time he was beginning to make money with his freighting business, she was too accustomed to her laundry business to give it up, even when he offered to support her for the remainder of her life. He snugged his hat down on his head and rode on, lost in his thoughts.

About eight miles from White Oaks the mountain ridges dropped off and opened out onto a broad basin. To the south he could see the buildings of Carrizozo and to the far west he could see a distant range of mountains. Between him and the western mountains, he saw a black slash of lava beds. The road gradually turned south and paralleled the line of stakes that marked the path of the future railroad.

Two hours after leaving White Oaks, he rode into Carrizozo. The town was no more than a store and a handful of houses, including one large home with a wide porch around it. At the store Virgil stopped long enough to get directions to Jack Parmaley's place from a couple of men whittling in the narrow shade of the roof overhang. With his knife, one whittler pointed out the large house. Virgil thanked him and rode on.

He turned west at the street, and soon saw the house. Though not a mansion, it was large and inviting, unlike Ed Keller's place in White Oaks. The wide porch gave the house a hospitable air. Virgil studied its wide windows and open doors as he dismounted from the mule and tied it to a hitching post.

Before he could take his first step on the stone path which led to the porch steps, he heard a voice calling out to him.

"Welcome!"

Virgil squinted at the deep shadows on the porch and saw an old man in a rocking chair. "Morning," Virgil answered. "I came to visit you, if you're Jack Parmaley."

"I was when I went to bed last night, and I don't think that's changed. Of course, you never know for sure when you get to be my age."

94

Virgil laughed.

The old man made an effort to get up.

"Keep your seat."

"Sonny," Parmaley said, "if I kept my seat as many times as people suggested, I'd be as useless as an old woman at a spitting contest."

As he reached the steps, Virgil removed his hat, then stepped up onto the porch just as Parmaley managed to get to his feet. Virgil was surprised to see a mattress on the porch.

"I sleep out here in the summer. It's cooler," he said, extending his hand. "I'm Jack Parmaley, and. . . ." He went silent for a moment. ". . . And, you're Rueben Child's boy, aren't you?"

Virgil felt his mouth drop open. He nodded, too shocked to respond.

"Why, you look just like him."

"Virgil," he offered. "Virgil Child's my name."

Parmaley grabbed Virgil's hand with his feeble grip. "And, your mother, Mary?"

"She died. That's why I'm in these parts, trying to find my father's grave and bury her beside him."

"I'm sorry to hear that, Virgil, but I'm glad to see you. We've got a lot of things to discuss."

8

Jack Parmaley ran his fingers through his thinning brown hair. His face was brown and etched with the wrinkles of years of working in the sun. Though he seemed unsteady on his feet, his eyes were as sharp and steady as his mind. He pointed to another rocking chair on the other side of the front door as he sat easily back down in his own.

Virgil grabbed the chair and pulled it in front of Parmaley. Removing his hat, he sat down and placed it in his lap. Parmaley picked up a small handbell on the table by his rocker and shook it vigorously.

Shortly, a housekeeper came out onto the porch. "Yes, sir," she said.

"We'd like something to drink. How about a glass of tea or lemonade," Parmaley offered.

"Tea," Virgil replied.

"Good for you! Lemonade's a girl's drink,

but I'll be damned if it ain't amazing to be out here in the middle of nowhere hundreds of miles from the nearest lemon tree and be able to have a lemonade. Once the railroad gets here, we'll be able to have ice brought to our door. Once I see that, I guess I'll have lived to see it all, yes sir."

"Would you care for anything else, sir?" the housekeeper asked.

"No, ma'am, just bring us our drinks and don't disturb us unless I ring for you."

"And, for your medicine."

Parmaley nodded reluctantly. "Things I didn't have to worry about when I was your age," he said to Virgil.

The housekeeper departed and Parmaley replaced the bell on the table. Then the old man began to rock the chair. "I suspect you want to know a bit about your pa."

Virgil nodded.

"He was a good man, Virgil," said Parmaley, a smile crossing his face. "We came to New Mexico Territory together, figuring on making our fortunes in ranching. Though your pa was twenty or more years younger than me, he was a good one, as dependable as sunrise, as honest as the day is long. Like me, he was from Texas originally, though I don't know much more about his background than that. We worked cattle there a few years after the war on the Four Jay Ranch out in the rolling hills. We knew we weren't going to make our fortunes working cattle for another man, so we came to New Mexico Territory to start our own ranches.

"Lincoln County was tough in those days, Billy the Kid and all his gang roaming around like a bunch of Apaches, but we minded our own business and claimed some land around here, you father around White Oaks and me between here and the malpais."

Virgil held up his hand. "Malpais?"

Parmaley nodded. "It's acres and acres of an old lava flow, black rock as sharp as a thousand razors. It'll cut a man to pieces quicker than a mountain lion. There's a single trail through it, which I marked out twenty or thirty years ago, but it's a place to avoid."

The door opened and the housekeeper came out with a tray. She handed a glass of tea to Virgil, then tapped her foot until Parmaley quit rocking his chair. When he was still, she sat the tray down over the arms of his rocker so he would have a place to keep his drink. There was a plate of sugar cookies on the tray as well. She picked it up and offered Virgil cookies. He took three, then watched her place three more on the tray in front of Parmaley.

"I want more than three," he said.

"Nope, three's more than you need today, but since you've a guest I'm being nice to you." She smiled and returned inside.

"She's trying to starve me, she is, she's trying to starve me," Parmaley said. "Now where were we?"

"Where did my father meet my mother?"

"El Paso, son, El Paso."

Virgil shook his head, wondering if his mother had indeed worked the brothels before taking up with his father.

"Rueben and I went to El Paso, where we had bought some Mexican cattle, to drive back up here to stock our rangeland. We met her there. She was cooking in a little eatery and Rueben and I fell in love with her. There weren't many white women in El Paso at that time, certainly not decent ones like your momma. But she was working in the eatery in the day and taking in laundry and ironing in the evening. She was saving up, planning on owning her own eatery, I think.

"She liked me, I know, but she loved Rueben. We were in El Paso three or four days and your pa ate every meal at the place where she worked. He promised her he'd build her a fine place to live and care for

99

her so she wouldn't have to work the rest of her life, just take care of him and their children.

"Mary was attracted to him, but just couldn't say yes, not on so short an acquaintance. She said for him to write her for a year and she'd give him an answer then. That's what your pa did, and one year to the day after she had told him how she wanted to do it, he wrote asking for her hand. She agreed.

"I rode with him to El Paso and saw him get hitched to her."

Virgil cleared his throat. "They were married before a preacher?"

Parmaley shook his head. "No sir, not before a preacher."

Virgil felt his spirit sag.

"They were married before a justice of the peace. It was all legal and such, your mother being that kind of woman. They came back and just over a year later had you. Your pa was proud as a puppy with two tails when you was born. Because of you and Mary, I know Rueben led a happy life until the day he died."

Parmaley shook his head and bit his lip. His eyes watered for a moment and he paused to sip at his tea and eat a cookie. "I still get emotional thinking about him."

100

Virgil looked away, trying not to embarrass Parmaley by witnessing his emotions. But he knew he had to ask a question, even if it would be hard on the old man. "Who killed my father?"

"I wish I knew for sure, son, because I'd like to have killed him for it. I didn't hear from Rueben for about three weeks — back in seventy-eight, I believe it was — so I rode out to his place. I found a grave and the burned-out ruins of your cabin. There were some prospectors about the area and I asked them about it. They said they'd come upon the cabin burned out by Apaches and one man dead and mutilated like the Apaches sometimes did. I asked them about a woman and kid, but they said they saw no sign of you or Mary when they stumbled on the place. There had been some Apache troubles, so it could've been true, the Apache taking women and children when they could. I searched for two months and saw no sign."

Virgil took a long sip of tea, then lowered the glass. "You think Apaches did it."

A tear rolled down the old man's cheek. He shook his head. "I did then, but I changed my mind later when I saw that the prospectors had taken over your pa's land. I think Ed Keller did it, him and his two

101

partners. They were rowdy types, with the morals of rattlesnakes. I had suspicions, but I didn't have proof."

After swallowing a sip of tea, Virgil asked, "Do you know where my father's buried?"

The old man nodded.

Virgil caught his breath. "Can you show me?"

"Not now, son."

"Why not?"

"It's buried over."

"Huh?"

"When Ed Keller started Deadman Mine, he buried the grave under his pile of tailings. There's tons of mine debris over where your cabin stood and where your father's buried."

Virgil cursed, then shook his head. "Momma asked to be buried beside him."

Parmaley shook his head. "It ain't possible anymore. She'd be happy knowing you brought her back to White Oaks. I offered to bring her back here once, but she refused."

"What!" exclaimed Virgil. "I thought you never found her after my father was killed."

"Eleven years later, son, I had business in El Paso. I ran into a cattle acquaintance that knew the both of us. He asked me if I knew she was in El Paso. I told him I didn't even know she was alive. I was as dumbfounded as a steer in a herd of heifers, and even more so after I visited her.

"You must've been in school that day, son, but I caught her doing laundry. She saw me and took to crying. I hugged her and gave her a kiss. She was genuinely happy to see me, until I asked her what had happened to Rueben. She didn't want to talk about it, no sir."

"Any reason why?" Virgil asked, putting his tea glass on the porch and leaning forward in his chair.

"She'd taken up religion and said vengeance was the Lord's. If she told me, she knew I'd kill them."

"Would you?"

"Damn straight I would have. I offered to bring her back to New Mexico and marry her. I made her the same offer that Rueben did — marry me and she wouldn't have to do any work except care for me, and I was in a position to live up to that promise by then, unlike your pa, who was just starting out when he made his promise. She refused, saying only that she didn't want to return to New Mexico until she died. Try as hard as I could, I couldn't get her to change her mind. She said if you lived out here you'd learn what happened to your father and try

103

to kill his killers. She didn't want her son to be a killer, even if her husband's murderers deserved to die."

Virgil slipped his fingers in his vest and retrieved the handkerchief. He unfolded it and handed it to Parmaley. "My mother gave me this the day she died. She told me the three splotches are my father's blood. The three names, she said, are men who would know where my father's buried."

"Your momma was a strong, righteous woman, son," Parmaley said as he squinted at the handkerchief. "I can't read without my spectacles. Who are they?"

"Ed Keller, Van McCracken and Tom Long," Virgil answered.

"Damn their hides," Parmaley growled. "I wish I'd found that out when I was young enough to do something about it. Are you planning on killing them?"

Virgil bit his lip. He wasn't sure what his plans were. He hadn't come to New Mexico to kill anyone, but that was before he knew what he knew now. With his father's grave buried under tons of mine waste, Virgil knew he was angry enough to kill them all. Even so, his mother had tried to screen him from blood vengeance.

"I don't know. I just don't know."

9

The return to White Oaks took the same two hours that the ride out had — it just seemed longer. Virgil Child carried a greater burden back to White Oaks than he had left with. Jack Parmaley had filled in pieces of his parents' lives that he had never known before.

His anger was red hot, and he didn't know whether it was because he had doubted his mother or because Ed Keller and his men had deprived him of knowing his father or sharing the mining wealth that could have given his mother a life of leisure rather than laundry. How could he ignore what the killers had done to the very flesh and blood to which he owed his existence?

He had come to White Oaks to bury his mother, not uncover her past. He had come to White Oaks to bury her beside his father, the one man she truly loved and loved truly. He could not do that now because his father was buried under a pile of tailings, tons of debris mined from the earth that had once been his own.

Rueben Child had gotten the tailings and Ed Keller, the bastard, had gotten the gold! On top of that, Keller had blasphemed Virgil's father by naming his stolen claim Deadman Mine. What was known as Keller Gulch should rightly be called Child Gulch. Keller had robbed Virgil not only of his fortune but also of his heritage. Virgil had only met Van McCracken briefly and he had yet to run into Tom Long, but he doubted he could hate either of them as much as he did Ed Keller.

When he finally came to the outskirts of White Oaks, he aimed the mule toward Deadman Mine and Keller Gulch. He rode all the way to the base of the mountain of tailings. Like a low, distant thunder, the machinery that crushed the ore rumbled in the mine works behind the tailings dump, which stood like a giant tepee beneath a wooden trestle.

Virgil stared at the mound of crushed rock. It was as worthless as a ton of Confederate dollars. His father was buried under tons of waste from a fortune that should have been his, a fortune that meant Virgil's mother would've been wearing fancy clothes

106

instead of laundering the sheets of prostitutes in El Paso. Virgil spat upon the rock as an ore cart clinked on the trestle's iron rails overhead and two miners dumped another load of crushed rock upon the pile. The gravel slid like a gritty curtain down the mound, some of it coming to rest on the ground before him.

"Damn you, Ed Keller," Virgil shouted, "damn you."

"What?" yelled one of the miners from above.

Virgil waved him away, then turned his mule back toward White Oaks. He passed the cemetery and decided that was where he would bury his mother. Even if he had found his father's grave, he wouldn't want his mother buried in land belonging to Ed Keller.

When he reached town, he would go to the funeral parlor and tell Tyrone Weatherby to see that a grave was dug in the cemetery for his mother. He wanted a temporary cross with her name upon it until the stone would be ready. And, he wanted another cross with the name Rueben Child upon it.

The long shadows of late afternoon were slowly melting away into the gray of dusk when Virgil turned down White Oaks Avenue and rode his mule to the front of the funeral parlor. This late in the day he half expected Weatherby's to be locked up, but through the window he could see a light coming from the storeroom. Maybe Weatherby hadn't gone home for supper yet.

Virgil jumped off his mule and quickly tied the reins to the hitching rail and stepped onto the walk. He twisted the doorknob and pushed the door open. "Weatherby," he called, "I need to see you."

As Virgil started down the hall toward the storeroom, the door flew open and the undertaker came out, ashen-faced and jittery.

"Vir-Virgil," he said, "I'm closed. I'll see you tomorrow."

"This won't take long," Virgil said as he strode up to Weatherby.

The undertaker spread his legs to block Virgil's advance down the hallway. "T-t-tell me what it is you need, Virgil."

Why was Weatherby so nervous? Virgil stopped opposite him. "Let me by."

"I'm closed," Weatherby insisted, "so get out."

"What are you hiding, Weatherby?"

"N-no-nothing," the undertaker said, his hands trembling like his voice.

Virgil pushed him aside, then stepped to the door and shoved it open. "Damn you,

Weatherby," he screamed when he saw the top of his mother's coffin standing on end against the side of her wooden box. He saw the stilled features of his mother's face as he stepped toward the coffin and the saw-horses which supported it. "What the hell are you doing, Weatherby?"

"N-no-nothing," the undertaker said.

Virgil spun around and glared at Weatherby trembling in the doorway. He stepped toward Weatherby and as he did, he caught a movement out of the corner of his eye, as if a shadow were rushing toward him. He saw a man in a black suit, his arm uplifted. Virgil spotted a wooden mallet in his hand.

He ducked instinctively, lifting his arm to protect himself, but it was too late. His brain exploded in a shower of light, and everything started to seem so near and yet so far away. Then, he felt himself falling; he seemed to fall forever, into a black pit that was silent and wet and hot.

When he came to, Virgil was confused. He did not know how long he had been unconscious, only that his head throbbed and that when he rubbed it more pain pulsed through his brain. He opened his eyes and was even more confused. Instead of a roof overhead, he saw a canvas of stars and sky. At least that's what he thought he saw, he was no longer certain. Last thing he remembered was questioning Tyrone Weatherby in the funeral parlor storeroom. Now he was staring at the stars, more than he had ever seen before. Then he saw not one but two crescent moons overhead and realized he was seeing double. He patted at what should have been a wooden floor, but his palm fell upon rocky soil. Then he realized he was sprawled upon the ground.

What was that nauseating smell? And why were his clothes wet? Had it rained? No, the ground was dry as a bone and the smell wasn't water. It was liquor! Now, nothing made sense. He heard something snort just beyond his head. He was so confused now, he didn't know whether to fear the noise or welcome it.

He rolled over onto his stomach and managed to push himself to his hands and knees, his head drooping between his shoulders as he tried to fight off the pain and dizziness that his simple movement had created.

Hearing the snorting sound again, he lifted his head and could just make out the silhouette of his mule, placidly grazing only a few feet from him. He didn't know what to think. He lifted himself to his knees and the world seemed to swim around him, the

110

stars becoming streaks rather than points of light. He took a deep breath, and his head felt like molten lava was burning above his left ear. He reached to touch the burning spot and felt a tender knot that sent pain pulsing all through the left side of his face. He groaned as he tried to stand, then sank back to his hands and knees and began to crawl toward his mule.

The animal stamped and snorted, then seemed to get Virgil's scent and calmed long enough for Virgil to grab the stirrup and hang on until he found the strength to pull himself up. He took a deep breath, the pain shooting through his brain again, then managed to make it to his knees. With both hands, he grabbed hold of the stirrup leathers and pulled himself up until he was standing on both feet and leaning against the saddle for support. He gathered his strength and poked at the stirrup with his foot, finally managing to slip his boot inside. Then, he took a deep breath and muscled himself into the saddle with his remaining strength. He hung on to the saddle horn with both hands and nudged the mule forward. For the mule's first few paces, Virgil swayed in the saddle, thinking he might fall, but somehow he held on, then got enough balance to reach for the reins. But he couldn't find them. He realized they were dragging on the ground. He cursed. He knew he had the strength to fall out of the saddle, but he didn't think he had the energy to pull himself back aboard.

The mule moved at its own pace and at its own direction. Virgil began to lean forward in the saddle, his head rolling back and forth with each step of the mule. He wasn't certain how long he had ridden that way or where he actually was when he heard a voice he recognized but could not immediately place.

"Whoa, fellow! What's the matter?"

Virgil reached for the reins which weren't there and mumbled, "Stop, mule." He heard competing hoofbeats and felt his mule jump into a trot, but only for an instant. A man on horseback rode up beside him and grabbed the mule's bridle, slowly bringing the animal to a stop.

"Phew, fellow, how much did you have to drink?" asked the voice.

For a moment, Virgil didn't answer, still trying to place the voice. He looked over at the man beside him, but could make out no features in the dark, only the orange point of a cigarette.

"How much did you have to drink, fellow?"

Then Virgil recognized the voice. It was Marshal Nap Webb. "I didn't drink nothing. I was attacked."

"Damnation if it ain't Virgil Child. Seems like I need to put you to bed to sleep all this off."

Virgil knew he wasn't drunk, but he wanted to sleep on his mattress back at the hotel so bad that he didn't argue.

Webb leaned over and grabbed the mule's reins. "Think you can ride a ways?"

Virgil nodded his head, but it hurt. He gasped, "I can."

He followed the marshal wherever he was going. When his mule came to a stop, he wobbled a moment until he felt the marshal's hands on his arm, helping him down from the saddle. When both feet were on the ground, Virgil draped his arm over the marshal's shoulder and together they marched to a darkened building. Virgil didn't know where it was and didn't care, just as long as he could get some rest to sleep away the pounding headache.

The marshal unlocked a door, then shoved it open. He moved cautiously about the room, which seemed packed with furniture. Then Virgil's shoulder bumped against an iron post or something and he felt himself being lowered onto a bed which was little

113

more than a blanket over a wood-bottomed bunk.

Virgil didn't care, he just wanted to sleep and try to get rid of that pounding in his head and the dryness in his throat. The last thing he remembered before falling off to sleep was a metallic clang.

Come morning the pain had eased, but the dryness tasted like sawdust in his mouth. He awoke a good while before he actually opened his eyes. He could tell it was day and he didn't want to expose his eyes to the brightness for fear that the pain would return. When he did crack his eyelids, the glare was overpowering and he closed them again. But in that brief moment, he saw something that angered him — jail bars. He was in jail.

He moaned for water, but received no reply. He cracked his eyelids again, squinting at the morning light. Except for him, the office was empty. He touched the still-tender knot on the side of his head and tried to remember how it got there.

After spending a few minutes adjusting to the light, he lifted his head to see if he was dizzy. Except for a touch of light-headedness, he seemed okay. He dropped his feet over the edge of the bunk and slowly sat up, planting his elbows on his knees and burying his forehead in the palms of his hand.

He sat like that until he heard a noise at the door. He looked up to see Marshal Nap Webb enter with a basket.

"Morning, Virgil Child. Did you finally sleep it off?"

"I wasn't drunk, Marshal. I was attacked by someone in Weatherby's Funeral Parlor."

"Suppose it was your mother?" Webb laughed.

Virgil kicked at the floor.

"I brought you some breakfast, if you can eat after as much liquor as you must've drunk last night. You smelled like a brewery when I brought you in."

"I want water."

Webb nodded and brought a bucket from beside his desk. He placed it against the cell bars. "There's a dipper in it."

Virgil stood up slowly, then wobbled the two steps to the bars. He bent over and took the dipper from the bucket and drank. The water was warm, but he didn't care. It went down like silk. He took a couple more dippersful, then stared at the plate of biscuits and gravy that Webb removed from the basket and shoved under the cell door.

"It's food, even if it is cheap. Now tell me what happened one more time. No lies this

115

time, Virgil."

"I went to see Weatherby. He was trying to hide something from me in the back room. Then somebody slugged me. That's all I remember."

"Thanks, Virgil. Now you just eat your breakfast and I'll be back in a few minutes."

Before Virgil picked up his plate and realized he had no fork or spoon, the marshal had escaped out the door. Virgil sat on the bed and ate with his fingers. He licked the plate of the gravy, then the stickiness from his fingers. The food felt good on his stomach. He wiped his fingers on the blanket.

When Webb returned, he was escorting Tyrone Weatherby. The undertaker seemed as nervous as he had the night before. Webb pointed Weatherby to a chair. "Sit," he ordered.

Weatherby slid meekly into place.

Webb stared at the undertaker. "Virgil says he came to see you last night and somebody slugged him when he was in your funeral parlor. That correct?"

"No, sir, not all of it, at least," the undertaker said. "He did come to my parlor, but he'd been drinking. He started sobbing about how he wanted to see his mother again. I tried to tell him no, but he wouldn't listen and threatened to whip me."

"That's a lie," Virgil shouted.

"Shut up, Virgil," yelled the marshal. "I listened to your story, and now I intend to listen to his."

Virgil nodded, the marshal's shout hurting his head.

Webb turned to the undertaker. "Now go on."

"I finally convinced him to go outside and come around to the back where I would let him in. Once I got him outside, I locked the door. I wasn't planning on letting him in the back door, but why he didn't just walk around the building I don't know. He managed to mount his mule and ride around to the back; I watched him out the back window. Something must've spooked his mule, though, because the animal darted off into the darkness."

Virgil grumbled. "How do you explain the knot on my head?"

Weatherby shrugged. "I guess the mule threw you."

The marshal turned to Virgil. "Just give it up, Virgil, trying to make excuses. The damn mule threw you. So what? It happens to lots of fellows. We damn sure won't tell anyone." He laughed.

"Can I go now?" asked Weatherby.

Webb nodded.

"Just a minute," Virgil said, standing up and marching to the bars. "I want to bury my mother in the cemetery. Go ahead and dig her grave, Weatherby. I'm not gonna look any more for my father's grave."

"It'll cost twenty dollars. The ground is rocky, so it'll be tomorrow before I'm done."

Virgil nodded. "That'll be fine. I told you I want stones for my mother and father. Until they're done, I want wooden crosses for the graves. Put their names on both, but on my father's paint 'Murdered in 1878.' "

The marshal shook his head. "You're only asking for trouble, Virgil, and I won't put up with it, not in this town."

Virgil didn't care what the marshal would put up with. The hunt for his father's grave was over. The hunt for his killers had just begun.

10

To save the town the cost of another meal, Marshal Nap Webb brought the local justice of the peace to the jail before lunch. Charged with public drunkenness, Virgil knew the accusations were false, but he also knew it was futile to fight them. After he pleaded guilty, the judge fined him fifteen dollars and admonished him never again to drink to intoxication in White Oaks.

Virgil wondered if the judge had ever heard of Van McCracken, but held his tongue as he slipped his fingers into his pocket for his money pouch. "I've been robbed," he gasped, drawing a jolt of throbbing pain through his head.

Marshal Webb stepped over to the jail cell, key ring in hand, and fumbled with the keys. "Hold your horses, Virgil. You don't think I'd leave you in my jail without checking your pockets. Your money and your pistol are safe in my desk." Settling upon the correct key, Webb shoved it in the lock and twisted it open.

"It's hard to remember," Virgil replied sarcastically, "being as drunk as I was."

Giving Virgil a sly smile, the marshal retreated to his desk, threw the key ring on a stack of wanted posters, then slid into his chair and opened the bottom drawer. He freed Virgil's money pouch and his pistol, placing them both on the desk.

Virgil stepped over, grabbed his pouch and loosened the drawstrings. He pulled out his wad of money and shook his head. He didn't have to count it up to know it was all there. Had money been missing, he could have strengthened his case that he was attacked the night before. He pulled off fifteen dollars and offered the fine to the justice of the peace. The judge grunted as his fingers wrapped around the money, then he turned and retreated out the door.

Webb leaned back in his chair and kicked his feet up on the desk near Virgil's gun belt.

"Weatherby said it'd be tomorrow before he got your mother's grave dug. You leaving town after she's planted?"

Virgil stuffed his money back in the leather pouch, then slipped it in his pocket. "I figure on staying a bit longer." Virgil grabbed his gun belt and buckled it around his waist, then pulled his pistol and checked the load. It was full.

"You won't be making any trouble, now will you?"

Shaking his head, Virgil slid the pistol in his holster. "Nope, I'm planning on staying sober from now on."

"Just keep away from Ed Keller."

Virgil stared at the sheriff's desk, then marched over to the jail cell, looking on the bunk, then under the bunk. "Where's my hat?"

The marshal shrugged. "Ain't seen it." He laughed. "It won't fit anyway, big as that hen egg is on your head. You ought to take a look at it." Webb pointed to an oval mirror hanging on a peg in the wall behind his desk.

Emerging from the cell, Virgil walked to the mirror. He grimaced at the knot over his left ear and at the purple of the bruise seeping down the left side of his face. His hair was matted in dried blood where he had taken the brunt of the blow. He turned and started for the door.

"Remember, Weatherby wants his money in advance. And don't you be threatening him the next time you see him, Virgil, or you'll wind up in jail again, only your stay'll be longer."

Without stopping, Virgil nodded and went out the door, closing it hard behind him. He squinted at the bright sunlight, his brain throbbing at the sudden brilliance as he stepped off the plank walk and headed to the hitching rail. His anger burned at a low flame when he realized the marshal had left his mule tied there all night without food or water. The mule's eyes were as listless as its drooping head.

He untied the mule's reins and led it to the nearest water trough. It drank greedily. Then Virgil climbed atop the mule and started down the street toward the funeral parlor, drawing the stares of several pedestrians as he passed. At Weatherby's he dismounted, tied the mule and went inside.

"Weatherby," he shouted, grimacing at the pain shooting through his head.

The undertaker, his hands trembling, stepped out of the back room. "You're not going to hurt me, are you?"

Virgil shook his head. "I'm sober now," he said, then pursed his lips in anger.

"You came to see your mother's coffin?"

Virgil let his hand slip near his gun belt, enjoying the panic in Weatherby's wide eyes, before reaching in his pocket and removing his money pouch. "You said you wanted twenty dollars in advance for digging the grave."

Weatherby nodded.

Virgil counted out the money. "Have you made the temporary crosses?"

Again Weatherby nodded. "In the storeroom, if you want to see."

Virgil advanced a step and Weatherby backed through the door, his eyes fixed on Virgil.

As he entered the storeroom, Virgil looked at his mother's coffin, still resting on a pair of sawhorses. Unlike last night, when he could've sworn the top had been removed, the coffin was now closed. He stepped beside it and saw that the lid was screwed on, but he noticed a couple scratches in the polished wood. Somebody had been tampering with the coffin for sure.

Weatherby backed into a corner and picked up a couple crosses, the names of Virgil's mother on one, the name of his father on the other.

"Paint 'Murdered in 1878' on my father's marker, like I told you," Virgil commanded as he peeled off another bill. "Here's ten more dollars for the markers. That should cover it."

Weatherby nodded.

"When'll you have the grave dug?"

"Tomorrow by three o'clock."

"Then I'll bury her at four o'clock."

Weatherby stood silently, watching Virgil.

"Go ahead, paint it now so I can take my father's cross with me," Virgil demanded.

Weatherby moved nervously to a work-bench and opened a can of paint. Taking a brush, he held it a moment to steady his hand, then began the task.

Virgil looked around the room, shaking his head. "Who hit me?"

"I don't know what you're talking about," Weatherby said without looking up.

"Somebody else was in here last night."

The undertaker said nothing as he painted.

"Why'd you open my momma's coffin?"

Grimacing, Weatherby glanced up at Virgil. The undertaker pursed his lips and shook his head. "You . . ." Weatherby paused a moment. ". . . were drunk."

Virgil slapped his hands together and Weatherby jumped as he moved to dip the brush in his paint can.

Weatherby's face paled and his hand trembled.

Virgil pointed at the coffin. "Is Mother still in there?"

The undertaker nodded. "Nobody touched her."

Drawing the back of his hand across his lips, Virgil studied the fear in Weatherby's eyes. "If I find out different, I'll take it out of your hide."

Weatherby nervously dipped his brush in the black paint, then continued lettering the cross.

Virgil stepped to his mother's coffin and grabbed a handle. He lifted the coffin enough to know it carried the same load that he had brought from El Paso. As he released the handle, he spotted a clump of felt on the floor between two empty coffins standing upright against the wall. He eased over to the coffins, then stooped and picked up a hat — his hat.

Spinning around with the hat in his outstretched hand, Virgil shook it at Weatherby. "How do you explain this?"

Weatherby's eyes widened. "It's a hat," he said, his voice dying meekly away as he averted Virgil's stare.

"Whose hat?" Virgil sneered.

Weatherby's hand trembled as he touched the brush to the marker.

Virgil flipped his hat over and studied the sweatband. He found a smear of blood that matched the location of the knot on the left side of his head. "How do you explain my

hat, Weatherby, if I fell off my mule outside?"

Without looking up from his work, Weatherby shrugged.

Gingerly, Virgil placed the hat atop his
head. He knew he had unnerved Weatherby,
and he knew that with a few threats he
could get the answers he was seeking. "Is it
gonna take all day to paint my marker?"

Weatherby shook his head, seeming relieved that Virgil wasn't questioning him
about the incident the previous night.
"About done, though it'll take a couple
hours for the paint to dry."

Virgil shook his head. "It won't matter.
I'll be taking it with me."

The undertaker stood back and looked at
the cross, then nodded and slipped the
brush in a can of mineral spirits. "Whatever
you say." Weatherby picked up the cross by
its arms and carried it to Virgil so he could
see the lettering.

"It'll do," Virgil said, "considering how
nervous you were." Virgil took the cross
from him, then laid the dry side over his
shoulder. "I'll be here at four o'clock tomorrow to accompany my mother to her grave."

"You want to carry her in your wagon?"

"Dammit, no. I want your hearse, all clean
and shiny."

"It'll cost extra."

"You'll get your pay when all's done. You just have the grave dug in time to drive her to the cemetery."

Weatherby sighed. "I'll work into the night, if that's what it takes to get that woman buried."

Virgil turned from Weatherby and marched down the hall to the front door and outside. On the street, he saw several men glancing at him and pointing at the cross on his shoulder. He turned the marker so men along the walk could read the freshly painted letters that told of his father's fate. After unhitching and awkwardly mounting his mule, Virgil turned the animal for the edge of town and the cemetery. Virgil felt the stares of many pedestrians.

At the street corner, Virgil realized a man on horseback had ridden up beside him to stare at the marker's lettering. The man said nothing after reading the cross, but eyed Virgil with a gaze as hard as granite. Wearing a black coat and string tie, the man had the look of a gambler about him. His hard gaze peered from the narrow slits of his slender eyelids and his cheeks and jaws were stubbled with whiskers. The man wore a well-oiled revolver on his hip, and Virgil figured him to be a man who had no qualms about using it.

Virgil nodded.

The stranger took off his hat as he read the inscription aloud. "Rueben Child, Murdered in 1878." His dark gaze shifted from the cross to Virgil's eyes. "You're Child's boy, aren't you?"

"Yes, sir."

"You look like him and your momma said you'd return."

"You knew my father?"

The stranger nodded. "I killed him. I'm Tom Long."

Virgil caught his breath in disbelief. Tom Long's name was written upon the handkerchief beside Van McCracken's and Ed Keller's. Virgil wasn't certain how to answer. Long seemed as dangerous and unpredictable as a coiled rattler. He might slither away or he might strike. Virgil felt a quiver in his hand and a racing of his heart.

"I figured we should've killed you and your momma the same day we killed your pa, but Ed and Van didn't have the stomach for it."

"Why you telling me this?"

Long flicked his whiskered cheek with his fingernails. "I figure you should know I ain't hiding from no one. I killed your pa, just like Ed and Van did. Ed'd deny it now, him

128

being too rich and respectable to have ever committed murder. Van, he's pickled his memory in whiskey and don't remember past his last bottle. They may be scared of you, but I ain't."

Virgil pulled the reins of his mule and the animal halted in the middle of the street. Long stopped his gelding, then turned the horse about to face Virgil.

"I came here to bury my momma beside my father."

Long's narrow lips parted in a slender grin that exposed teeth yellowed from cigarettes. "His grave's gone."

"Beneath the tailings at Deadman Mine."

Long nodded, then laughed. "Ed named the mine for your pa. Ed sure thought it was funny. He never figured you'd return. I always knew you would. Your ma was strong stock and when she said you'd come back for us, I knew she'd raise you on the bile of revenge. I should've killed the two of you right then. It's one of the few mistakes I ever made."

"Why you telling me all of this?"

"I believe in putting all the cards on the table. Ed'll try to convince you he had nothing to do with it and save his respectable hide. I've made a decent living all these years by reminding him he was involved in your pa's murder. It was a memory he didn't like, once he turned respectable."

"You don't seem to be bothered by it."

"That was a good while ago." Long pointed his index finger at Virgil's nose. "If you try to take any of us, you best go for Ed and Van first because up against me, you'll wind up as dead as your pa."

Virgil felt the chill of the ice in Long's veins. "I came here to bury Momma."

Long laughed as he lowered his finger. "Say what you want."

"But," Virgil admitted, "the more I learn about my father's death, the more I want to settle the score."

"I admire a man that's honest, even when he as much as says he plans on killing me."

"It didn't start out that way," Virgil said as much to himself as to Long.

"It never does, it never does," Long said, then stared hard at Virgil. "Just one piece of advice."

Virgil met Long's hard gaze with as stern a stare as he could muster.

Long pointed to the cross. "Have the undertaker make you a marker with your name on it. You'll need it if you tangle with me." Long spat between their mounts, then jerked the reins of the black gelding and galloped back up the street, whistling shrilly.

Virgil sat motionless on his mule a moment before nudging the animal with his boot heel and starting him toward the edge of town. He passed the cemetery, then angled up the hard-packed road that led to Deadman Mine. Halfway up the road, he reined the mule toward the giant tailings pile just as a couple miners on the trestle above the waste heap emptied another ore cart. The finely ground rock slid down the pile like a gravely veil.

Drawing up at the foot of the pile, Virgil dismounted and dropped the reins. The mule stamped nervously at the rumble of the mine works as Virgil carried the cross to the base of the tailings and shoved it into the gravel. He looked around and strode over to a rock the size of a loaf of bread. He grabbed the rock and returned to the cross. After extracting the cross from the gravel, he held it upright with his left hand as he hoisted the rock with his right and let it fall upon the head of the marker, driving its pointed bottom into the hard, rocky earth. After a couple hits, the cross had enough of a toehold in the ground that Virgil could release it. He grabbed the rock between both hands and began to pound it against the head of the cross. Slowly, Virgil drove the cross deep enough into the ground that it stood straight and steady.

"Hey," came a shout from above, "what are you doing?"

Virgil looked up at the trestle, where the two miners stood glaring down at him. Virgil waved and both men held a hand to their ears so they could hear his response over the rumble of the mine machinery. "Posting a sign for Ed Keller," he yelled. "This is Deadman Mine, isn't it?"

Both men nodded.

"Then let your boss know so he can tell Keller."

The men shrugged, then grabbed the ore cart and started pushing it back to the mine works.

Virgil strode over to his mule, took the reins and mounted. He aimed the animal for the hard-packed mine road and followed it to the main road. As he neared the cemetery, he saw Tyrone Weatherby carrying a pick and shovel among the graves. Virgil guided his mule toward the cemetery. As he approached, he called Weatherby. The undertaker flinched, then spun around, dropping his shovel and pick.

"You surprised me."

Virgil eyed him warily. "You digging the grave yourself?"

Weatherby's head bobbed up and down

like a cork on rough waters.

"As many miners as there are in town, I figured you'd hire one or two of them to do this work for you."

Weatherby shook his head. "They cost too much."

The undertaker didn't like to let go of a dollar, Virgil decided.

Weatherby pointed to a vacant plot of ground. "This good enough for your mother?"

"As long as there's room for fine headstones for her and my father."

Weatherby bent over and picked up the shovel. "I'll start now. I even brought a lantern so I can work after dark."

Virgil nodded. "Fair enough." He turned the mule back toward White Oaks and left Weatherby to his work.

In town, Virgil stabled the mule with instructions for it to receive extra feed, then walked over to the hotel. He stopped at the desk and asked the proprietor to have some water heated and a tub brought to his room so he could bathe.

Ozanne nodded. "Will do. Just give me thirty minutes, maybe less."

Virgil backed away from the desk.

"Don't leave," Ozanne said, looking under the counter and pulling out an envelope.

"This came for you this morning. Ed Keller's housekeeper brought it over."

Virgil took the envelope and headed up the stairs. Reaching his room, he unlocked the door, then slipped inside, tearing open the envelope after he kicked the door shut with his foot.

He read the note aloud. "Meet me tonight after dark in the front of the hotel." The note was signed by Priscilla Keller.

What could she possibly want, he wondered.

11

Though his head still ached, Virgil Child felt better after finishing his bath and an afternoon nap. Changing into clean clothes and eating a full meal in the dining room made him feel almost whole again, except for that knot on the side of his head.

After finishing a dish of apple cobbler and his third cup of coffee, he left the dining room and took to a chair in a shadowy corner of the front room as he awaited Priscilla Keller. He was uncertain what to expect from her. She was pretty, but she was also a Keller and he couldn't be certain she was trustworthy. He hoped she took after her mother rather than her father.

He waited for a half hour after dark and was about to give up on her when he saw the door swing open. She marched inside, looking quickly back and forth. Her gaze alighted on Virgil as he arose from his chair. She seemed both relieved and frightened.

As Virgil emerged from the deep shadows, her mouth fell open and her hand instinctively reached to cover it. "What happened? You're so bruised."

"Somebody hit me."

Priscilla looked nervously around. "Please, we must hurry before someone sees me."

"Who?"

"Anyone who might tell my father."

Virgil placed his hat gently upon his head, took her arm and steered her outside. She was jumpy until they stepped beyond the squares of lamplight that seeped from buildings.

"My father would kill me if he knew I was seeing you."

"Why you doing it then?"

"I don't understand what's going on. Father's always been tough, though mother was able to take some of the starch out of him. You, though . . . when you arrived it really made him jumpy. He hasn't been the same. What's this all about?"

Virgil pondered whether to answer her question. Could he trust her?

"And, for the last two nights father was out after dark, something he doesn't do for fear somebody'll rob or kill him. I asked why he was about, but he told me to mind my own affairs."

Wordlessly, Virgil walked beside Priscilla. His silence seemed to draw her closer to him. They reached the end of the street before Virgil spoke. "You scared?"

"Unsettled."

Virgil stopped and stared to the west. His eyes focused on a yellow glow of light a quarter mile away. He realized a lantern was burning at the cemetery and remembered the undertaker's promise to work late on his mother's grave.

"Would you walk with me to the cemetery?"

She leaned her head against his shoulder and nodded. "Sure. It gives me peace to see Momma's grave. I've gone there once a week since I lost her. I don't think Father's been there a single time, though he passes by there on the way to and from the mine."

Virgil detected the bitterness in her voice, but felt inadequate to address it. They walked silently for several minutes.

Above them the sky was splattered with stars. Behind them a crescent moon was just rising, casting a pale glow over the land.

Finally, Priscilla lifted her head from his shoulder. "Are you a bad man? That's what my father says."

Surprised by the question, Virgil pondered before answering. "I guess all men have a

137

little bad in them, though I've never killed anyone or robbed anyone, if that's what you mean."

"You frighten Father unlike any man I've ever seen, save maybe Tom Long. Now *he's* a bad man."

As they neared the cemetery, Virgil could hear the thud of pick against rock and the metallic scrape of the shovel as it emptied more of his mother's grave. He mulled over Priscilla's question, but she seemed to read his mind.

"I'm not saying you're a bad man. How could someone who brought his mother all the way from El Paso to bury her in White Oaks be a bad man? I just don't understand what's happened since you came."

Virgil shrugged. "Maybe your father's conscience bothers him."

"About what?"

Virgil ignored her question as they approached the cemetery. Priscilla started toward the obelisk that marked her mother's grave. "I want to talk with Weatherby," he said. "You stay by your mother's grave and I'll join you."

Virgil pulled his arm from hers and moved quietly toward the grave. He saw the top of Weatherby's head bobbing up and down as he swung the pick and chipped away at the hard earth. Glancing behind him, he saw Priscilla with bowed head at her mother's grave. Easing up to the side of the grave, Virgil watched Weatherby switch the pick for the shovel, then move the lantern out of the way. The undertaker took a deep breath as he slid the shovel's blade beneath a pile of loosened rubble, then lifted it with a grunt and tossed it out of the grave to the side opposite Virgil.

Weatherby emptied three full shovels of rubble and was going for another when he evidently caught Virgil's profile out of the corner of his eye. "Aaaah," he cried, throwing down the shovel and ducking instinctively from the newly realized threat.

"I just came to see how the grave was coming along."

The undertaker released a deep breath. "Wish you'd said something." He panted as he tried to catch his breath. "I decided to finish it tonight so you could bury her sooner if you wanted."

"That's mighty square of you, Weatherby."

The undertaker smiled and bent to pick up his shovel. "I won't charge you any extra, either."

Virgil squatted down over the grave, his right hand sliding the pistol from the holster at his side. He cocked the hammer and pointed the gun at Weatherby's head.

The undertaker's smile disappeared when he looked back up into the malevolent eye of Virgil's revolver. He gulped.

"I've a few questions I want answered, Weatherby."

The shovel slid from the undertaker's hand and clattered as it struck the pick. Weatherby trembled.

"I wasn't drunk last night and you know it."

Weatherby offered Virgil a blank stare.

"I want answers," Virgil growled. "I could shoot you and bury you here tonight and no one would be the wiser."

Weatherby gulped again.

"Now, who hit me last night?"

The undertaker's mouth opened but no words came out.

Virgil shook the gun at his head.

"Keller did it," Weatherby said.

"Why'd you have the top off my momma's box?"

"Keller had to see for himself if she was a woman he remembered from the early days."

"Was she?"

Weatherby nodded. "He kept saying, 'It's her, it's her,' until we heard you come in."

"You didn't disturb her, did you?"

Shaking his head vigorously, Weatherby answered, "No, no, no. I wouldn't do that."

"Did Keller tell you how he knew my momma?"

"No," Weatherby said. "He didn't say much. He was too rattled."

Releasing the hammer, Virgil lowered his pistol and slid it into his holster. "Don't tell him about our conversation, Weatherby."

"No, sir, I won't," Weatherby assured.

"I'll see you tomorrow before four o'clock for the ride to the cemetery."

"Yes, sir. I'll be glad to get her buried for you." His voice and hands were trembling.

Virgil stood up and bit his lip. There across the grave stood Priscilla Keller, staring at him.

Not knowing how much she had overheard, he strode around the grave, took her arm and steered her out of the cemetery. "I told you to stay away." Virgil felt her arm quiver in his hand. "What did you hear?"

"Everything, but I don't understand why he attacked you and what your mother has to do with it all."

"Last night, I went to the funeral parlor and saw my momma's coffin open. Before I could get answers, I was hit on the head. Weatherby says it was your father that did it."

141

"But why would he hit you?"

"He was tampering with my mother's coffin."

"But why?"

"He wanted to make sure the woman in the coffin was the same woman he remembered when they first met years ago."

"It still doesn't make sense."

Virgil grimaced. He didn't want to reveal too much to Priscilla because she was, after all, still Keller's daughter. Even so, he felt a kinship with her because she had had no more control over her parents' actions than Virgil had had over his.

"It doesn't make sense," she repeated.

Virgil shook his head. "It does if you believe he and his partners killed my father."

Priscilla began to cry.

As they walked back to the hotel, Virgil explained the blood saga of the handkerchief. "Your father's been scared all these years that I would return and kill him."

"Is that what you intend to do?" she asked.

Virgil walked a couple minutes without responding. "I came here to bury my momma by my father. She told me the men whose names were on the handkerchief would know where he was buried. I pieced together that the names were also those of his murderers."

"It still doesn't make sense. Why wouldn't Father help you find your father's grave?"

"Priscilla, your father got rich on land that would've been my father's had he lived. Your father, Van McCracken and Tom Long took my father's life and what should've been his fortune."

She hung her head and pulled her arm from Virgil's grasp.

"Deadman Mine got its name from my father. His grave is buried under tons of mine tailings. What is known as Keller Gulch should've been Child Gulch."

"No, stop, please, don't tell me any more. What do you want now?"

Virgil shrugged. "I'm not sure what I want, not until I get Momma buried."

They walked silently the remainder of the way into town and shortly found themselves back in front of the hotel. Virgil wanted to assure her he had nothing against her. In fact, he felt a growing kinship to her.

"Ozanne has some good apple cobbler. I bet we could sweet-talk him out of some, if you're hungry."

She shook her head. "No, I best be getting back. I've already spent too much time away from home. If Father finds out, I'll be in bad trouble, especially if he learns I was with you."

They stepped toward the hotel and a rectangle of light seeping out of a front window. Just as they were fully under the lamplight by the hotel signboard, Virgil heard a commotion at the other end of the walk, and then a loud shout.

"There you are, you dead son of a bitch."

The voice had a vague ring of familiarity to it.

On instinct, Virgil shoved Priscilla to the walk and fell atop her. She screamed just as an explosion ripped through the air, followed by a second shot. Virgil winced with pain as he rolled off Priscilla and jerked his revolver from his holster. He squeezed off a shot toward his assailant.

He glimpsed the attacker jump behind the corner of the hotel, then he heard retreating footsteps. Jumping to his feet, Virgil scampered to the end of the walk, turned the corner of the hotel, and fired blindly into the night. He ran to the back of the hotel, peering into the darkness. Seeing nothing, he retreated to the front of the building, where Priscilla lay upon the walk, dazed.

"What's going on?" Ozanne yelled from inside.

"There's been trouble," Virgil answered as he dove for Priscilla, his hand falling upon a moist red spot staining the sleeve of her blouse. He knelt beside her, touching her arm. She cried in pain.

"She's been shot," Virgil yelled. "She's been shot. Somebody get a doctor."

Virgil cursed. Had Priscilla led him to an assassin? Had Ed Keller sent her to set him up? Those were answers that could wait until she had been attended to. "Will somebody go for a doctor?" he screamed.

12

Sitting on a bench in the marshal's office, Virgil grimaced as the doctor dug into his arm with a pair of tweezers, trying to fish out one of the three pieces of shot that had struck him during the ambush. The doctor, a young fellow who had finished medical training and then come west because of his asthma, pinched a fold of flesh on Virgil's arm, trying to keep the lead from working its way deeper into his muscle.

Virgil grimaced, then gasped at the pain. "You sure Priscilla's gonna be okay, Doc?"

"Worry about yourself until I dig all this lead out," the doctor commanded.

Virgil glanced at his arm and saw threads of dried blood extending from three tiny holes. He felt faint for a moment and looked away, then gasped as the doctor jerked the tweezers out. He heard the click of something hitting the floor.

"Damn," said the doctor. "I dropped it."

He studied the floor, then gave up. "I know I got it. That's the last one." He dropped his tweezers in his black bag and pulled out a bottle of liquid. He dampened a cloth, then rubbed it over each tiny wound, squeezing the cloth so the liquid seeped like burning lava into each hole.

"Both you and the girl were lucky," said the doctor. "She had one shot in her arm. It bled badly, but looked worse than it was."

"Shut up, Doc," demanded Ed Keller. "It's none of his concern." Keller turned to Virgil. "What the hell were you doing with her?" His face reddened with rage.

"Calm down now, Mr. Keller," chided Marshal Nap Webb. "I'll get to the bottom of this."

"You damn well better, Marshal, or I'll see someone else gets your badge."

Now Webb's face turned red and he slapped at his shirt. At first Virgil Child thought the marshal was going to turn his badge over to Keller, but instead the lawman fished the cigarette makings from his pocket and began to construct a smoke.

The doctor wrapped cloth bandages around each wound, then patted Virgil on his good shoulder. "Get some rest when the marshal's done with you. The soreness'll be gone in a couple days. Keep the wound

147

clean and it'll heal just fine." The doctor closed up his black bag and turned to the marshal. "Anything else?"

"Not tonight," the marshal replied.

The doctor nodded. "Good night, gentlemen." He opened the door and disappeared into the darkness.

Webb lit his cigarette, then nodded at Virgil. "What were you doing with her?"

Virgil lied to protect Priscilla. "I walked to the cemetery to check on Momma's grave. On the way back I ran into her." Virgil sat on a bench opposite Webb's desk. The lawman rested on a desk corner he had cleared. Behind the desk Keller paced back and forth like a caged animal. Virgil knew the only thing that was caged was Keller's anger.

"You got any proof?" Keller demanded.

Virgil licked his lips. "Ask Tyrone Weatherby if I was out there. He was still digging the grave. We had an interesting talk about me being drunk and throwed from my mule." Virgil grinned.

Keller's eyes narrowed. "What did he say?"

"The truth, Keller, the truth."

Keller's hands knotted into fists and he stepped around the desk. Virgil shot up from the bench, prepared to defend himself.

148

"Stop it, dammit," ordered Webb as he stuck his tobacco pouch back in his pocket, then rolled his cigarette. "I don't care what happened last night. As far as I'm concerned, Virgil, you fell off your damned mule while you were drunker than a skunk. I want to know about tonight and who shot Priscilla Keller."

Virgil shrugged. "I was minding my own business, walking with Priscilla, when some fellow called me a son of a bitch. I saw sudden movement and fell on Priscilla as a shotgun went off once, then again. I shot back, but lost the man in the dark."

"What were you doing with Prissy?" cried Keller.

Virgil stared at Keller without responding. He found it odd that Priscilla's father was more interested in what he was doing with Priscilla than in who actually shot her. Could it be that he knew who had tried to assassinate him? Keller seemed too obsessed with the answer to his question for him to have sent Priscilla to draw Virgil into an ambush.

"Who shot me, Keller?"

The mining magnate's hands knotted into fists again. "What are you suggesting?"

Virgil shrugged. "I'm not as dumb as you think."

149

"You're not as rich as I am, either."

Virgil laughed as he stood up, retrieved his shirt and poked his good arm in the sleeve. "I could've been as rich, Keller, if my father had lived."

Keller sneered. "I don't know what you are talking about."

"What are you two discussing?" Webb asked, lighting his cigarette and exhaling a cloud of smoke.

Virgil grimaced as he shoved his wounded arm in his sleeve, then began to button the shirt. "I met Tom Long today."

"Tom's a liar," Keller shot back.

"You don't even know what he said."

Scratching his head, Webb got up from the corner of his desk. "What are you two talking about?"

Both Virgil and Keller ignored the marshal.

"Tom Long said my father was buried at your mine beneath all the tailings."

"How the hell would I know where your father's buried?"

Virgil nodded. "Because you killed him."

Webb spun around and stared at Virgil. "What did you say?"

"You heard me, Marshal."

Keller pointed his finger at Virgil. "Lies, all of it's lies. You're just coming here to try and take my fortune."

"Like you stole it from my father."

Webb stared at Virgil. "Those are powerful words you're throwing about. You got any proof?"

"Nothing you'd believe, Marshal, except the handkerchief, and it can't talk."

"Then maybe you'd better not talk any yourself, Virgil, unless you've got proof that'll hold up in a court of law," said the marshal.

Virgil looked from the marshal to Keller. "The law may not be on my side, but the truth is." He grabbed his hat from a peg by the door. "If there's nothing else, Marshal, I'd like to retire."

Webb shrugged. "If you didn't get a look at your attacker, there's not much we can do."

"You might ask Keller who he paid to assassinate me." Virgil opened the door and stepped outside into the darkness. He left the door open as he started toward the hotel, and heard the door shut behind him. At the end of the block, he turned the corner and paused, staring back down the street at the marshal's office. Though he was tired, he played a hunch, figuring to wait until Keller left to be sure the mine owner headed for his home. He glanced behind him and saw the lamplight seeping from an upper window of the Keller mansion. It was the window he remembered as Priscilla's when she'd watched him leave after his first meeting with her father.

Virgil waited almost half an hour, wondering what Keller and the marshal could be talking about or what they were plotting against him. His energy was sagging when he saw the door open and caught a brief glimpse of Keller in the light before the door closed. Virgil squinted against the darkness, trying to make out Keller's form as he came down the street. Virgil heard his footfall on the plank walk, then nothing. As he peeked around the corner, he saw Keller crossing to the opposite side of the street and heading north instead of south toward his home.

Letting out the breath he had been holding, Virgil smiled to himself. Perhaps his hunch had been right. Quietly, he crossed the street, clinging to the darkness and avoiding any light cast on the street as he followed Keller past saloons lit with activity and other buildings darkened with sleep. Keller walked to the north edge of town without ever turning around or indicating he had a single suspicion he was being followed.

Twice Virgil feared he had lost Keller. The

first time he heard a stray dog bark at the mine owner's approach and was able to spot him. The second time, Keller vanished, but the glow of lamplight soon appeared behind the murky window of a small shack. Keller had apparently slipped inside.

Virgil circled wide of the one-room shack and approached it from the windowless backside, where light glowed between the edges of the rough-hewn lumber that had been used for the shelter. As he neared the shack, he heard Keller's angry voice.

"You damned fool," Keller cried. "You almost killed my daughter. Would have if that bastard hadn't knocked her to the ground and fallen on her."

"I didn't mean to," whined a voice Virgil recognized as that of Van McCracken, the drunk and former partner of Ed Keller.

"Do you want me to cut off your liquor, Van?"

"No, no, Ed, not that. I need it. I need it bad."

"Then you better not shoot at him again when someone else is with him. Do you understand?"

"I do, just don't take away my liquor."

Keller laughed. "That's what I'm gonna do, Van."

"Please don't, please!" pleaded Mc-

Cracken.

"I'll restore your liquor account once you've killed him, but I'll take it away again if you ever say I put you up to this."

"I wouldn't do that, Ed, really I wouldn't, but I don't know how I can kill him."

"Try it tomorrow night. You know he's staying at the Hotel Ozanne. I found out he's in room number seven. After midnight, slip inside with your shotgun and kill him in bed."

"Then will I get my liquor back?"

"You sure will, Van, as long as you never mention my name as being involved in any of this."

"Thank you, Ed, thank you," McCracken gasped.

Virgil heard the door slam and caught a glimpse of Ed Keller starting down the hill toward town and his mansion.

The lamp was blown out in the cabin and all was quiet for a moment, until Mc-Cracken started sobbing about needing his whiskey. It was disgusting that a man could crave a drink so much that it turned him into a whimpering baby. Virgil was sickened at the sound, but waited for twenty minutes just to give Ed Keller an adequate start.

By the time Virgil reached the hotel, he was exhausted. He climbed up the stairs, unlocked his room, entered and locked the door behind him, but didn't light a lamp. He undressed and pulled back the covers and fell into bed, wincing at the pain from his left arm and the still-sensitive knot on his head.

He wondered about Priscilla, hoping she would be as well as the doctor had indicated. He wondered what she thought of him after he had revealed so much about her father's past.

Though he was exhausted, he had many things to think about before tomorrow. He had to get a new suit to wear to his mother's burial. Then, he had to devise a plan to keep himself alive.

He didn't trust the marshal enough to tell him what he had overheard. This was business Virgil would have to take care of himself.

More than anything else, Virgil remembered his mother on her deathbed, wanting to be buried by her husband. He had promised her he would do that, but he had failed.

He had promised her he would not seek revenge. It was another promise he would have to break. If he didn't, he knew he would be lying beside her in the cemetery.

13

Virgil Child slept until midmorning, then dressed and went downstairs for something to eat. Herb Ozanne had stopped serving breakfast by then, but offered him some cold biscuits and bacon from the kitchen.

"Any idea who shot you?" the hotel proprietor asked.

Virgil shrugged. "I couldn't identify him."

Ozanne tugged at his earlobe, then nodded. "Hope they find him quick. You were lucky the way the shotgun blasted my sign. It'd killed both of you had it caught you full bore."

"Do you lock the outside doors at night?"

The proprietor held up his hands. "What good would it do? We leave the windows open to catch the breeze in summer. Anybody that wants in could crawl inside. That's why I paid to put locks on the room doors."

"Just checking, since someone's out to get me."

"I don't blame you."

Virgil nodded. "I'll bury Momma this afternoon. Could you heat water and bring a washtub to my room for a bath this morning?"

"Sure thing," Ozanne said, pointing to the platter of leftover biscuits and bacon. "Have all you want." Ozanne left to draw water.

After eating his fill, Virgil walked through the dining room, past the front desk and out the door. He studied the wall and the hotel signboard. The chest-high sign had been obliterated by the shotgun blast. The brick wall itself was blackened and gouged out where a load of shot had hit.

As Virgil studied the wall, he understood how he and Priscilla had taken so few pieces of lead. The full blast had hit the sign and the brick wall behind it, with only a few pieces of lead ricocheting downward where he had covered Priscilla.

He retreated back inside the hotel, shaking his head at how lucky he was to be alive. He wondered if he would survive this night were Van McCracken to come calling, but at least this time he would be prepared. He returned to his room, then waited for Ozanne to bring him hot water for the tub, which had already been delivered.

Once Ozanne brought the water, Virgil bathed and shaved as best he could, his left arm being stiff and sore, then dressed and buckled on his gun belt. Taking his hat, he peeked out into the hallway for a moment, looking for Van McCracken. Satisfied that nothing was amiss, Virgil headed down the hallway for the stairs and out the door onto the street. He studied every pedestrian and rider who approached as he made his way down the street toward Reed's Mercantile. Business was slow, and two clerks greeted him as he walked inside.

"I need ammunition and oil for my revolver," Virgil announced, "and a suit of clothes if you have some ready-mades."

One clerk pointed him to a rack of clothes and the other said he'd get ammunition. Virgil tried on three suits, none of which fitted him perfectly, and selected one that was a little tight around his muscled shoulders. He picked out a shirt, suspenders, tie and socks, then spent twenty more minutes choosing a black felt hat from several that fit nicely upon his head.

As he moved with his armload of clothes to the counter, he passed the room where the liquor barrels were kept and heard a voice he recognized as Van McCracken's.

"Just a jiggerful is all I want," McCracken pleaded.

"Not until Mr. Keller says he'll pick up the cost again, Van," replied the clerk. "You know the rules: if he closes your account, you have to pay for it."

"But I'm broke," McCracken pleaded.

"That's not my problem," the clerk answered.

Virgil stepped up to the counter, dropped his pile of clothes, then turned around to face McCracken as he came out.

The drunk strode out of the room, saw Virgil standing at the counter, then jumped back inside.

"No you don't," said the clerk. "Now get out of here."

"I'm scared," McCracken said. "That man out by the counter, why, he's dead."

The clerk poked his head out of the liquor room and shrugged. "You're a damn drunk and about as worthless as they come. Now get out of here." The clerk shoved McCracken out.

McCracken braked hard and backed away from Virgil.

A clerk called out, "I've got ammunition and oil for your piece. You need anything else?"

Virgil grinned at McCracken. "Just something to shoot at."

McCracken broke and ran for the door, flinging it open and running out into the street, then disappearing from view.

The clerks laughed. "Wonder what got into him," said the one nearest Virgil.

"Guess he saw a ghost from his past," Virgil answered.

After paying his bill from his money roll, Virgil gathered his purchases and left the store, looking carefully around for Mc-Cracken. Not seeing the drunk, Virgil returned to the hotel and climbed the stairs for his room.

He spent the next hour checking and oiling the revolver, getting the feel of it in his hand. Just before Ozanne quit serving lunch at one thirty, Virgil went downstairs to eat. "Whatever you've got left will be fine," he told the proprietor.

Ozanne brought him the butt end of a roast, boiled potatoes, red beans and cold bread. Virgil ate quickly and silently, then returned to his room and dressed for his mother's burial. The last thing he put on was his gun belt and newly oiled revolver.

He stared at himself in the mirror. He felt uncomfortable in the fancy clothes, but a man only buried his mother once and, when he did, he needed to show proper respect.

Even though he was dressed, Virgil reclined on the bed, hoping the rest would ease the pain in his arm and the throb in his head. The afternoon dragged by, seeming to take months before the time finally rolled around. Standing up, he patted the gun at his side, grabbed his new hat and checked both directions before stepping out the door into the hall.

At the head of the stairs, he studied the two strangers seated in chairs near the hotel desk, then started for the door. Neither man showed much interest in him. Outside, he gauged every passerby as he strode the two blocks to the livery stable. He had a stable hand saddle one of his mules, then mounted and pointed it down the street for Weatherby's Funeral Parlor.

Virgil was pleased to see the hearse out front, its brass fixtures glistening in the bright sunlight. Through the glass in the side of the hearse he could see his mother's coffin. It had been a long journey for her from the foot of the Jicarillas to El Paso and back. It had been an even longer journey for him.

He didn't pay any attention to the covered buggy parked behind the hearse until he drew even with it and a voice called his name.

"I'm glad to see you're okay."

Virgil grabbed his hat and removed it, smiling at Priscilla Keller. "Shouldn't you be resting in bed?"

"Probably," she nodded, "but I figured I'd pay my respects to the mother of the man who saved my life last night."

"Your father know about this?"

She looked away from Virgil. "I'm eighteen. He doesn't control everything I do."

"I'm just worried what he might do to you."

She shrugged. "I'm not worrying about him anymore. I'm gonna start living my life the way I want."

Virgil nodded. "Thank you for coming."

"I guess my family at least owes you a little respect."

"I thought that was all history, but your father's forcing me into a corner. When that happens, I'll fight back. I hope you won't hold it against me."

Priscilla smiled. "My mother always taught me to look at what was right and lead my life that way. Would you care to ride with me? My arm's still sore and you could steer my horse better."

Virgil dismounted and tied his mule to the hitching post. "My arm's stiff too, but between us maybe we can manage two good

162

arms to the cemetery and back." He crawled into the buggy and took the reins.

She leaned against his arm.

He grimaced. "My bad arm."

Priscilla apologized. "I didn't mean to hurt you."

Virgil laughed. "It wasn't that bad. Your being here has made me feel better than anything since my mother died."

"Funny," Priscilla replied, "but I've felt the same way around you."

Virgil appreciated Priscilla. A woman who would come to the funeral of a woman she never knew could not have set him up for an ambush the previous night. Virgil gave a satisfied nod. She was cut from a different cloth from her father.

The door to the funeral parlor opened and Tyrone Weatherby emerged, dressed in a black longcoat and black hat, his face somber and sullen. He looked at Virgil and nodded. "Are you ready?"

"I am," Virgil answered.

Weatherby moved to the front of the hearse and climbed into the seat, taking the reins. Shaking the leather lines, Tyrone started the hearse toward the cemetery, carrying Mary Child on her last journey.

Virgil pulled out behind Weatherby. As the hearse advanced down the street, several men took off their hats and paused until the coffin passed. He studied the men, searching for Van McCracken in case he decided to make his move earlier than Virgil figured. Virgil never saw McCracken, but he did catch a glimpse of Tom Long, staring with his narrow, evil eyes and not lifting a finger to remove his hat.

Priscilla saw Long and tightened her hand around Virgil's sore arm. When she realized what she had done, she released her grip. "I'm sorry, but that man scares me. He was once my father's partner."

"I know," Virgil answered.

They said nothing more until the hearse turned off the road onto the short trail to the cemetery.

"A big crowd came to bury my mother," Priscilla said. "She was generous and caring, and the folks around here loved her. My father'll only attract the curious when he dies."

Virgil tugged on the reins and brought the gray gelding to a halt beside the hearse. Weatherby climbed down and swatted at the film of dust upon his black coat, then opened the back of the hearse as Virgil stepped down from the buggy and helped Priscilla to the ground.

Weatherby motioned for Virgil to take a

position on the opposite side of the coffin. Together the two men dragged the coffin from the hearse and carried it past the tombstones and markers toward Mary Child's unfilled grave.

At the grave, the two men lowered the coffin onto a pair of boards laid across the hole. When both men straightened, Weatherby looked at Virgil. "Is there anything you want said, her being your mother?"

Virgil grimaced. He hadn't thought of any fancy words. She had been his mother. She had borne him and raised him, mostly on her own. Words were inadequate to repay that debt. Virgil shook his head. He didn't know what to say.

Then, Priscilla stepped to his side and took his good arm. "May I say something, a prayer?"

Virgil nodded.

Priscilla smiled, then bowed her head. "Only one of us here today knew the woman we are about to bury, but she must have been a good woman, for she raised a good son. She will be buried here near others who were good of heart and spirit. We commend her soul to you, dear God, so that one day we may all rejoin our mothers in your Holy House. Amen."

"Amen," Virgil said. "Those were fine words."

Weatherby nodded, then removed his coat and draped it over a nearby stone marker. "It'll take two of us to lower the coffin."

Virgil slipped out of his coat and started to drape it over a tombstone.

"I'll hold it for you." Priscilla took it from him.

Weatherby retreated to the hearse and returned with four lengths of rope, each with a metal hook on the end. He tossed two at Virgil, who snagged them from the air. "Slip the hooks under the handles and we can lower the coffin into the grave." The undertaker turned to Priscilla. "When we lift the coffin up, pull the boards from under it, would you please?"

"Certainly," Priscilla said, stepping toward the grave and bending beside the coffin.

When Virgil and the undertaker had attached their hooks, they lifted the wooden box and Priscilla quickly pulled the slats from beneath it. Then, Virgil and the undertaker lowered Mary Child into the ground. The coffin settled on the bottom of the grave, then the hooks slipped off the handles and Weatherby and Virgil extracted them from the grave.

"I'm sorry, Momma, sorry you're not

closer to Father's grave," Virgil said as he tossed the ropes back to Weatherby, "but you can see his resting place from here."

With that, Virgil turned around and stared at the tailings dump across the road and down Keller Gulch. Then he squatted and picked up a handful of White Oaks' rocky soil and tossed it down upon his mother. "You brought the temporary cross, didn't you, Weatherby?"

"It's strapped onto the hearse. And I brought an extra shovel in case you want to help cover her."

Virgil nodded. "That would be fine."

Weatherby retreated to the hearse, pulled two shovels and the wooden cross from atop it, then returned. He gave a shovel to Virgil and the cross to Priscilla.

Together the undertaker and the son of Mary Child began to cover her grave. The work went fast, and when they mounded up the earth over her coffin, Priscilla stepped forward and offered the cross to Virgil.

Taking the wooden marker from her, he stepped to the head of the grave and began to drive the cross into the newly turned earth with the head of his shovel.

As he hit the top of the cross and it plunged into the soil, he heard the sound of a galloping horse from down the road. The hoofbeats grew louder, and then Virgil heard a shout. He turned around and saw Ed Keller charging down the mine road, then heading straight for the cemetery.

Virgil shoved the spade into the ground and watched Ed Keller cross the main road and aim for the cemetery. Keller charged past the hearse and buggy and dodged tombstones as the horse crossed into the cemetery. Keller held something over his head like a spear.

Virgil's hand fell to the butt of the revolver at his side.

Keller reined up the horse not fifteen feet away, then threw two pieces of wood upon the grave.

Virgil saw the broken cross with his father's name on it and felt a surge of anger pulse through his veins. He wanted to kill Ed Keller. He might have done so, were it not for Priscilla Keller beside him.

14

Ed Keller's face was contorted with rage and he pointed his finger like a pistol at Virgil Child's nose. "A couple miners said you planted that cross on my property. You stay off my land."

"It wasn't always your land," Virgil shot back.

Keller turned to his daughter. "What the hell are you doing out here, Prissy?"

Priscilla lifted her chin defiantly. "I came to visit Mother's grave."

"Then why are you holding his coat?" he challenged.

"It seemed the decent thing to do, like visiting Mother's grave. When was the last time you stopped here?"

"I see it every day."

"From the road," Priscilla answered, "but you never stop."

"That don't matter, Prissy. I've told you to stay away from Virgil Child and I want you to mind me, you hear?" He jerked his head toward Virgil. "You ain't been nothing but trouble since you arrived in White Oaks, Child."

"You're the one that started the trouble when you killed my father, Keller."

"It's true, Father, isn't it?" screamed Priscilla.

"Shut up, girl! It's a lie."

Virgil scoffed. "Tom Long says it's true and he was there."

"Tom and Van McCracken, they're the two that killed him. I didn't have anything to do with it. I tried to stop them, but they wouldn't listen."

"It won't wash, Keller. You were all in on it. You've been buying McCracken off with liquor so he'd never mention it. Tom Long's been threatening for years to tell folks exactly how you became owner of the Deadman and you've been paying him off, too."

"Is that true, Father, is it?"

"Shut up, Prissy. Get in your buggy and go on home."

Virgil shook his head. "If it weren't true, Keller, why did you have Weatherby open my momma's coffin? You recognized her. You knew she was the wife of the man you murdered."

The undertaker grimaced. "He held a gun

on me, Mr. Keller, and threatened to kill me if I didn't fess up."

Virgil stepped toward Keller. "Then, when I came in unexpected, you slugged me and tried to make it look like I was drunk. Why didn't you just kill me then? Or is it that you just hire other people to do your dirty work since you became rich on the blood of my father?"

Keller spat at Virgil's feet. "You came here to kill me."

Virgil felt the hate rising in him like bile. "I came here to bury my momma. Before she died, she told me not to seek revenge."

"You're lying, Child. Why the bloody handkerchief then?"

"Momma wanted to be buried by her husband. She told me the men on the cloth would know where he was buried. That's all," Virgil said. "I didn't start out to kill you, but I guess your conscience is going to drive me to it."

Priscilla began to weep, and tears streamed down her cheeks. "I'm glad Mother's not alive to see this. Did she know?"

Keller shrugged. "It don't matter, Prissy."

"It does to me."

Keller's shoulders sagged like his defiance. He bit his lip, then stared hard at Virgil. "I've put men on guard at the mine. I've told them to shoot you on sight if you step on mine property."

"Father," screamed Priscilla, wiping at her tear-filled eyes and wet cheeks, "how could you do that?"

"Shut up, Prissy," Keller said, his voice a sinister growl. "You've had an easy life because of the things I did."

"You think this is easy?" She stepped toward Virgil. "I'm sorry." She handed him his coat. "I'm going home now to think."

Virgil took the coat from her. "Thank you for the kind prayer."

She dabbed tears from her eyes, then waved limply to Virgil. "I'd like to see you again, discuss a few things."

"No," shouted Keller. "You stay away from him."

Priscilla strode past her father and toward the buggy outside the cemetery grounds. "I'm eighteen and old enough to make my own decisions."

"Not if you want to sleep under the best roof in White Oaks, Prissy."

"I told you not to call me Prissy," she yelled back over her shoulder. The hurt that had previously tinged her voice had been replaced by anger.

Keller spat in disgust, then waved his hand at the undertaker. "Weatherby, you best climb atop your hearse and head back to town so Virgil Child and I can have a word together."

Weatherby nodded. "Whatever you say, Mr. Keller." The undertaker moved to pick up his shovels.

"Forget the spades, dammit, and go. I'll buy you new spades if that's what it takes to get your carcass on that hearse and moving."

Weatherby turned to Virgil. "My pay for the funeral?"

"Go on, dammit," shouted Keller. "I'll pay double anything he owes you."

The undertaker scampered past Keller and scrambled up into the hearse's seat. He rattled the reins and turned the hearse in a tight circle before heading back down the main road toward town.

Keller eyed Virgil. "You should've taken the money I offered you and left White Oaks the day you arrived."

"Not everyone can be bought, Keller."

"You won't leave White Oaks alive, Child."

Virgil shook his head. "Did you hire someone to ambush me the other night? I know you damn sure didn't have the courage to try it yourself."

Keller's face reddened. "Let me show you something, Child," the mine owner said, slipping his hand very slowly under his coat. Virgil watched the coat bulge as Keller's hand reached his armpit. After a moment's hesitation, Virgil realized Keller was going for a gun in a shoulder holster.

Keller jerked his forearm from his coat.

Virgil saw a clump of black metal in Keller's hand and froze for a moment.

Keller swung his pistol toward Virgil. "I'm no coward."

Without time to draw his own gun, Virgil flung his coat at the mine owner.

The coat fanned out toward Keller, upsetting his aim and his mount. The black gelding snorted and reared on its hind legs as the coat flew by its head.

Virgil lunged for the animal and Keller as a gunshot punctuated the air.

"Damn you, you bastard," Keller shouted as he jerked the reins and tried to control the terrified horse.

Virgil grabbed Keller's gun arm, clamping his wrist in an iron grip until the pistol tumbled to the ground. Then Virgil pulled Keller out of the saddle.

Keller landed hard on his shoulder and rolled over into the slashing legs of the panicked gelding. The animal kicked him in the shoulder. Keller screamed, then rolled into a tombstone in an attempt to retrieve

174

his gun. The gelding darted between Virgil and Keller.

With the agility of youth, Virgil dodged the horse, darted to where the pistol had landed and kicked it away with his boot. He spun around and kicked Keller in the stomach as he tried to climb to his hands and knees. Keller grabbed a tombstone to steady himself, then gasped for breath and collapsed on the ground.

Virgil pounced upon him, planting a knee in his back, then grabbing his hair and jerking his head up. Keller squirmed in pain as Virgil growled in his ear. "You best thank Priscilla, because she's the only thing that's keeping me from killing you right now. You're not the man you were when you killed my father, and don't you forget it."

Virgil shoved Keller's face to the ground, crushing his nose in the rocky soil. He went over to Keller's pistol, picked it up and shoved it in his belt. Everything had happened so fast, he didn't have time to think about the pain pulsing along his left arm and the sore side of his head. Then, as he caught his breath, he felt the ache throbbing through his left side. For a moment he felt weak and unsteady, but the pain subsided as his breathing slowed.

Keller groaned and rolled over. His face

was splattered with blood and dirt and his eyes were wide and terrified as he stared at the blue sky overhead.

"You better get out of my sight, Keller, before I decide to whip you again," Virgil shouted.

Keller managed to make it to his hands and knees, then grabbed a tombstone to steady himself before trying to stand up.

Virgil sat on a stone marker as he watched Keller get to his feet. The mine owner tottered for a moment, then staggered toward his horse, which had stopped to gnaw on a patch of yellowed grass. Virgil glanced at the horse to make sure Keller couldn't pull a carbine on him, then watched the mine owner grab the reins and pull himself aboard. He started back to town, cutting across the rocky terrain to reach the road.

Virgil watched him reach the edge of town, then turned his attention to his mother's grave. He picked up the shovel and tapped her temporary wooden marker a bit farther into the soft soil. He bent over and grabbed the second shovel Weatherby had provided and saw the broken marker that had been his father's cross. Virgil leaned the shovels against his mother's marker, then grabbed the pieces of his father's. Keller had only pulled the crosspiece from the marker, bending the nails. Virgil found a rock and beat the bent nails straight enough that they would fit in the holes in the other wood piece. Then, he pounded the two pieces back together and planted his father's cross in the soft corner of his mother's grave. Taking a shovel, he beat the cross into the soil. This would work until the permanent marker arrived.

If his mother and father weren't buried side by side, at least their markers would be together. Virgil grabbed the second shovel, retrieved his coat and started walking back to town, sorry that he hadn't tied his mule behind Priscilla's buggy when he came out to the cemetery.

He took his time, trying to save his strength; his fight with Keller had taken a lot out of him. After a bit, the two shovels grew cumbersome. He tried carrying them military style on his left shoulder, but the wounds from the shotgun made that too uncomfortable. He wanted to carry them on his right shoulder, but knew he must keep his right hand free in case he needed his gun. So, he just gritted his teeth and marched on, holding both shovels in his left hand. He found himself short of breath by the time he reached Weatherby's Funeral Parlor.

The door was locked but through the display window he caught a glimpse of Weatherby. He knocked on the door and stood by the window where Weatherby could see him. The undertaker came to the front and opened the door.

"Here's your shovels. How much do I owe you?"

Weatherby took the shovels, and put them inside the door. "In addition to what you've already paid, twelve dollars will do it — fifteen dollars if you want me to cover the grave with rocks."

Virgil fished his money pouch from his pocket and counted out twenty dollars. "There's a little extra to make sure the grave's attended."

Weatherby took the money and nodded his head. Then he looked up at Virgil. "Maybe I don't deserve an answer, but did you come here to kill Ed Keller?"

"I came here to bury my momma."

"Keller thinks otherwise."

"It's his conscience finally getting the best of him after all these years. He's the richest man in all of White Oaks, and I figure he couldn't enjoy his money for the worry that one day I'd come looking for him. Odd how life works out, isn't it?"

Weatherby grinned. "Not as odd as how

death works out. The whole town turned out for his wife's funeral. There wasn't a person about that didn't like her, save maybe Tom Long. Keller's gone to seed since she died. Once he dies, there may not be twenty people see him planted."

Virgil nodded. "Thanks for taking care of Momma."

The undertaker lifted his handful of money. "This is thanks enough."

Virgil turned around and strode to the hitching rail, where he untied the reins of his mule. He mounted and rode toward the livery stable. He left the animal with a stable hand and walked back outside, ready to go to the hotel for some supper. He was tired and knew he needed a good night's sleep, but he figured Van McCracken would be visiting him with his shotgun, at least if the drunk had been sober enough the night before to remember his conversation with Keller.

As he approached the hotel, he saw that Herb Ozanne had removed the sign splintered in the shotgun attack. Ozanne was replacing it with new lumber. When the proprietor heard him approach, he turned around and nodded. "You've got a visitor waiting inside," he said.

Virgil hoped it was Priscilla Keller.

"Marshal Nap Webb wants to talk to you."
Virgil gritted his teeth and entered the
hotel.

15

The moment Virgil Child walked into the hotel, Marshal Nap Webb shot up from the chair where he'd been sitting smoking a cigarette. The marshal exhaled a cloud of smoke that obscured his eyes for a moment, then stepped toward Virgil.

"Ozanne says you wanted to see me."

Webb nodded. "There ain't been nothing but trouble since you got to town."

"I didn't start it. I came to White Oaks to bury my momma."

"She's buried now, so why don't you just ride on out of White Oaks and the territory."

"I would have, Marshal, had Keller and the others left me be until I could bury Momma. When I arrived in White Oaks, I didn't have any debts to settle other than finding my father's grave. Problem is, I made too many people nervous. Keller's tried to buy me out or intimidate me through you. Somebody's tried to ambush me. Now I've got some debts to pay, and I won't be leaving until they're paid up."

"Whipping Keller at the cemetery ought to settle one debt."

Virgil shook his head. "I couldn't even bury Momma without the man that killed her husband riding up and disrupting it."

"There's no proof Keller killed your father."

Virgil shrugged. "He along with Van McCracken and Tom Long shot him. Tom Long admitted as much to me, and theirs were the names on the handkerchief."

"A bloody handkerchief don't prove that."

"I came here thinking those three might know where my father was buried, if any of them were still alive. They were all alive, and apparently scared of me. I figure it was one of them that tried to ambush me. And, Keller just pulled a pistol on me at the cemetery."

The marshal drew deeply on his cigarette, then pulled it from his mouth. "That's not how Keller described it."

"He's lying."

"Keller says he came to visit his wife's grave when he saw Miss Priscilla there. He says you attacked him."

"He must've been drunk and fallen from

his horse like me," Virgil said sarcastically.

The marshal pointed the cigarette's burning end at Virgil. "I don't know what happened at the cemetery, and I've only got his word against yours."

"That hasn't stopped you before from siding with him, Marshal." Virgil reached for his waist and pulled Keller's revolver from under his gun belt.

The marshal flinched and dropped his cigarette, then slapped at his own revolver before he realized Virgil was offering him the gun. Webb sighed, then bent down and picked up his cigarette.

"This is Keller's pistol. He kept it in a holster under his arm. He pulled it on me at the cemetery, but I took it from him." Virgil grinned. "After he fell off his horse."

Webb grabbed the gun and studied it. "It's Keller's all right. He packs it when he carries large sums of money about town."

"Return it to him with the warning that I'll kill him if he ever sticks his hand under his coat again."

"I ought to arrest you, but it's getting suppertime and I'd just have to feed you. That costs the town money."

"I'll be here tomorrow, if you change your mind," Virgil shot back.

"It'd be a hell of a lot simpler if you'd just leave."

"Let me tell you this, Marshal: Keller's trying to get me killed. I don't know that he pulled the trigger, but he was behind the shotgun attack that almost killed his daughter. He or someone else will come for me until I'm dead or they are."

Webb stuck the cigarette back in his mouth and barged past Virgil for the door.

Virgil watched him out the door, then turned to the stairs and went up to his room. He fell on the bed to rest in the dying light of day. The ceiling darkened as he relaxed there, thinking how to protect himself if Van McCracken attacked tonight. He'd sleep on the floor or sit in the chair in the corner all night. A drunk like McCracken would surely think he was asleep in bed and attack there, allowing Virgil to shoot back before he realized his mistake.

As dusk gave way to darkness, Virgil sat up, ran his fingers through his hair and headed downstairs for supper. He moved to the corner and the only empty table in the dining room, sitting with his back to the wall so he could see whoever entered. He patted the gun at his side as Ozanne took his order. Once his supper came, he realized the true depth of his hunger. Virgil had eaten three bowls of hot stew and five corn-bread muffins, and was about to attack a slice of cherry pie, when he glanced at the doorway and saw Priscilla Keller standing there.

He lifted his arm and she saw him, a smile washing over her face. She started for him, twice looking over her shoulder as if she feared her father might be following her.

She sat down at the table.

"Did you and Father fight?"

Virgil nodded.

"He says you hit him with a shovel in the face and knocked him out of the saddle."

"He's lying. He pulled a pistol from his shoulder holster. I knocked him off his horse before he could shoot me. I took the pistol and turned it over to the marshal."

Priscilla buried her head in her hands. "I don't know who or what to believe anymore. He's my father."

"And I'm a stranger."

She nodded her half-hidden head. "I don't know what to do. Maybe I should leave home and move into the hotel."

"You can't stay here. It would look bad."

"I don't care."

Virgil bit his lip. "I do."

Priscilla lifted her head and peeked over her hands at Virgil. "But why?"

"It's hard to say."

She smiled at him.

"I don't know how all of this is going to work out, but I'd be . . ." He paused, uncertain if he could really say what he wanted to.

"Go on," Priscilla urged him.

"I'd be interested in seeing you, if you agreed."

"I would," she replied without hesitation.

Virgil felt a frown slide down his lips.

"What's the matter?" she asked.

"I just don't know that it could work out. I don't see any way out of the differences between me and your father."

Priscilla's face darkened too. "I know. I want to believe him, but every time I ask him something, he treats me like an ugly stepchild. Even so, he's still my father."

Virgil pushed the plate of untouched cherry pie away. "I know. That's what bothers me about even thinking of seeing you. That and the fact I don't know it's safe for you to be with me in White Oaks."

"And you think my father's behind that?"

Virgil looked deep into her pleading eyes, but he could not tell her the truth. It might drive a wedge between them. If she ever learned the truth, it would be better for her to learn it herself rather than be told by him.

"I think the same man who tried to ambush us the other night is planning to try for me again tonight."

She gasped. "You know who it is?"

Virgil nodded. "I think so."

Priscilla leaned across the table. "Who? Is it my father?"

"I don't think so, but I can't name the man until I know for certain."

She took his hand. "You can trust me."

"I know, but if I was wrong *you* might never again trust *me.*"

Priscilla's downcast eyes made Virgil uncomfortable.

"Shouldn't you get back home before your father realizes you're gone?"

"I don't care. I'm not taking his orders anymore. Would you escort me home?"

"I can't, Priscilla."

Her eyes filled with hurt. "But why not?"

"I almost got you killed last night. Until we find out who's been shooting at me, I best not accompany anyone out in the dark."

"It'd be okay," she pleaded.

"No. Maybe tomorrow, but tonight you should go on home alone."

Her lip trembled and her eyelids fluttered as she pulled her hand from his. "The house just isn't the same with Mother gone."

What could he say? He felt sorry for her

and wished he could take her in his arms and protect her from all her worries, but he had enough of his own for a while. "Please," he said, "go home and get a good night's sleep."

Reluctantly, Priscilla arose, drawing the stares of several admiring men. "Be careful," she whispered.

"I will. Now you run along."

Priscilla walked across the room as pretty as a dream, then disappeared out the door.

Why was it never easy? Why couldn't he have met Priscilla and courted her without having to face the shadow of her father's past? Virgil wondered how he could avoid telling her that her own father had been behind the assassination attempt on him and — by accident — her.

He pulled the plate of cherry pie in front of him and stared at the generous slice of dessert. He ate a couple bites, then toyed with the pie, wishing things were simpler with Priscilla, wondering if Van McCracken would come tonight. Tossing his fork down on the pie plate, Virgil stood and pulled enough change from his pouch to cover the meal, then dropped the coins on the table.

As he left the dining room, he studied the empty hotel entrance and bounded up the stairs, making sure the hall was empty before pulling his key and entering room number seven. He locked the door behind him, then lit a lamp. He pulled off his broadcloth coat and undid his tie, tossing them both over the foot of the bed. Next he unbuttoned his collar, then slipped his boots off and left them on the floor by the bed.

Ozanne had left on the washstand the newly washed clothes Virgil had worn the night before when he had been shot. He unfolded the shirt and took his pillow from the bed, then stuffed the pillow into the shirt. Pulling back the covers on the bed, he placed the bloated shirt at the head of the bed. Next he took his clean britches and stuffed them with a blanket he rolled up from the end of the bed. He shoved the britches up against the bloated shirt. In the light, the decoy was obvious, but in the dark Virgil figured it would throw McCracken.

Virgil then moved the room's rocking chair to the corner opposite the bed. He unbuckled his gun belt and laid it on the floor beside the rocking chair. Next he blew out the lamp. Then he retreated to the chair. Sitting down, he bent over and pulled his revolver from its holster. He then straightened and leaned back in the rocking chair, holding his gun in his lap, ready for a visit from Van McCracken or anyone else.

There was nothing to do but wait, and Virgil knew it could be a long wait. He found himself thinking of Priscilla, a young woman he had just met a few days previous, and about his father, a young man he didn't remember but apparently resembled, according to the reactions of Ed Keller, Van McCracken and Tom Long.

Occasionally, he heard footsteps in the hallway and he tensed up, waiting for McCracken to kick open the door and attack, but each time he heard men opening other rooms.

Then all was silent and he took to wondering whether his mother would be satisfied with her grave, even if she wasn't resting beside her husband. He wondered what she would think of him waiting to ambush one of her husband's killers.

Now and then he caught himself dozing off and he shook his head to stay awake. He managed to last for an hour and a half after midnight. Then, despite his hardest efforts to stay alert, he dozed off. A couple times he shook himself out of his drowsiness at a suspected sound at the door, but nothing ever came of it. The deeper into the night he went, the less he fought the sleep, which dragged him down for longer and longer periods.

His sleep, though, was suddenly shattered by a tremendous explosion at the door.

He shook his head and grimaced at the smell of gunpowder. He saw a shadow enter through the shattered door.

The shadow seemed disoriented, waving a weapon in the air.

Virgil lifted his pistol at a shape he knew had to be Van McCracken.

McCracken stepped toward the bed and laughed like a maniac. "Now I'll kill you for sure," he shouted.

Virgil cocked the hammer on his pistol.

The shadow lifted his shotgun and stuck it on the mattress.

Virgil took aim, just waiting for McCracken to pull the trigger.

A flash of light and an explosion bounced around the room after McCracken pulled the trigger again. "You're dead now, you son of a bitch," McCracken called gleefully, then spun around.

"No I'm not," yelled Virgil.

He squeezed the trigger and another shot rang out. McCracken toppled to the floor as the shouts of men echoed down the hall.

16

The hallway was full of spectators when Marshal Nap Webb pushed his way into the room. He looked at the splintered door, the blackened sheet and the gouged mattress, then at the body face-down on the floor. He toed at the dead man with his boot before squatting over him to get a closer look.

Virgil Child waited in the rocking chair.

"It's Van McCracken," Webb announced, then stood up and looked at Virgil. "What happened?"

"Self-defense," Virgil replied, "and there's no way you can make anything else of it but that, Marshal."

Webb scratched his chin, then reached for his cigarette makings in his shirt pocket. "Tell me what happened."

"I was sitting in my rocker when he blasted inside. He pointed that shotgun at my bed and fired. I shot back."

Webb examined the bed, picking up the

192

remnants of the decoy. "Looks like to me you might have been expecting company."

Virgil nodded.

"Why didn't you tell me?"

"You wouldn't have believed my story. For all I know, you might even have tipped Mc-Cracken off."

A couple fellows eased into the room, but the marshal spun around and told them to clear the hallway. After much grumbling, the crowd dispersed.

"McCracken's the one that shot Priscilla and me," Virgil added.

"How do you know tonight what you couldn't answer before?"

Virgil stood up and walked to the door. He glanced into the hall to make certain it was clear. "After I left your office, I trailed Ed Keller. Instead of going home, he headed to McCracken's shack. Keller jumped Mc-Cracken for almost killing his daughter, then threatened to cut off McCracken's whiskey ration at Reed's Mercantile unless he got me tonight while I slept."

Webb shook his head. "Serious accusations you're making against this town's most prominent citizen."

"It's the truth."

"You should've come to me," Webb repeated as he finished his cigarette, then

193

dropped it on the floor and crushed it with his boot.

"I might not be alive if I had."

"But why would McCracken want to kill you?"

Virgil shook his head. "Best I can figure it, I look like my father and it haunted him."

"Don't bring your father's death into this. It's not related."

"No, Marshal, it's the cause of all this."

"Damnation," Webb said, then called down the hall for Herb Ozanne.

The hotel proprietor arrived at the door quickly.

The marshal ordered him to fetch Tyrone Weatherby to take McCracken's body.

Virgil arose from his rocker and sat his pistol on the washstand, then bent over at the foot of the body and picked up the sawed-off shotgun that twice had been used against him. He looked at the stock, then at Marshal Webb. "You know who this belongs to?"

Webb shook his head and shrugged. "Not an idea."

"Neither do I," replied Virgil, studying the stock and two letters carved in the wood. "Do the initials 'EK' mean anything to you?" Virgil couldn't help smirking at the marshal.

194

"Not offhand," Webb replied.

"EK as in Ed Keller. Is that not a possibility?"

The marshal gave Virgil a hard stare. "The initials don't prove anything. It could've been stolen or someone else's initials."

Ozanne poked his head in the room. "Weatherby will be here in ten minutes." He shook his head at the damage. "Virgil, I guess I'll have to move you into room twelve. It's the only vacant one left until I get this door fixed and a new mattress."

"Obliged," Virgil replied, before turning to the marshal. "Any other questions? If not, I'm retiring to my new room."

"Just don't leave town."

Virgil grinned. "Earlier you wanted me to leave, and now you want me to stay. Can't you make up your mind?"

Webb frowned.

After gathering his belongings, Virgil moved down the hall to his new room. He undressed and quickly fell into bed, and slept soundly into the next morning. He knew he had slept too late for breakfast, but he put on his clothes quickly and headed downstairs. He was surprised to see Priscilla sitting stiffly in one of the chairs.

She jumped up from her seat and bounded across the room to greet him. "You're okay,

Virgil." She flung her arms around him. "I don't know what to say."

"You've said enough."

"Was it who you thought it would be?"

Virgil nodded. "It was. Van McCracken."

"I know," she said, lowering her face and speaking softly. "Did Father put him up to it?"

What could he say? The truth was too dangerous for Priscilla, but he could not lie either. So, he said nothing.

Priscilla hung her head. "You answered my question without saying a thing."

"I'm sorry, Priscilla." Her arms slid from around him. Like her, Virgil didn't know what to say or do. Before he or Priscilla said anything else, Virgil saw Marshal Nap Webb enter the hotel.

Webb immediately spotted Virgil. "Good, you're up, Child. I need you to come with me to the office." Webb stopped in his tracks when he realized who was with Virgil. "Miss Priscilla, you shouldn't be associating with him."

"I pick my own friends."

"Your father won't be too happy about this."

"I'm not a kid anymore," she shot back.

"That's not what I meant."

Then, Priscilla turned, wrapped her arms

196

around Virgil and kissed him full on the lips.

Virgil knew she was just trying to shock the marshal, but he enjoyed it anyway.

Priscilla spun about and strutted past the marshal.

Webb stood admiring her figure and the bounce of her red hair until she disappeared out the door. Then he turned back to Virgil. "Why don't you come with me down to the office?"

"Am I under arrest for anything?"

"No, sir, I just want to get a few facts straight."

Virgil held up his hand. "Give me a moment to see if I can scrounge something out of the kitchen, since I missed breakfast."

Webb nodded his approval.

Herb Ozanne gave Virgil three cold biscuits to eat on his way to the marshal's office.

Webb opened the door and Virgil went in, surprised to see Ed Keller sitting in the marshal's chair, drumming his fingers on the marshal's desk.

Keller jumped up from his seat and started cursing. "You bastard, spreading rumors that I had McCracken try to kill you."

"You did, Keller. I followed you night before last to McCracken's. I heard you telling him to do it or you'd quit buying his liquor."

"Liar," Keller yelled, stepping toward Virgil.

Marshal Webb intersected him. "Calm down, Mr. Keller."

"Tell the marshal how I took your gun from you at the cemetery yesterday," Virgil replied. "Tell him how you pulled the gun on me, tried to kill me."

"Bastard," screamed Keller. "I was returning that cross you erected on my property."

"Whose property was it originally?" Virgil shot back.

The marshal looked from Keller to Virgil. "What cross?"

"I'll tell you the one," Keller shouted. "The one that's got his father's name painted on it, along with the words 'Murdered in 1878.' That's the one."

Webb's eyes narrowed at Virgil. "What were you doing on his property?"

"Planting the marker as close as I could to my father's grave."

"Where is this grave you're talking about?" the marshal asked. "We can just dig it up and see for ourselves."

"No you can't," Virgil answered. "Keller's buried it under tons of tailings from the Deadman Mine."

Keller pounded his fist into his palm. "That's a damned lie."

Webb cursed in frustration and dug out his cigarette makings. "I don't know which one of you to believe."

"You damn well better believe me if you want to hold on to your job as marshal."

Webb scoffed. "Before Child here came to town, I might've been scared, but no more, Mr. Keller." The marshal rolled his cigarette, then shook his head. He glanced up at Virgil. "Getting back to McCracken's death, there's one thing I don't understand."

"What?" Virgil replied.

The marshal licked the cigarette paper and folded the moist edge over the tobacco. "If Keller had arranged for McCracken to attack you in the night, why would he have pulled a gun on you the afternoon before?"

"You'll have to ask him. He's the only one that knows."

Keller grinned. "The reason is I never pulled a gun on him, Marshal. I threw the cross down and next thing I knew, Child was rushing me, pulling me from my saddle and trying to beat me. He got in a couple good licks and grabbed my gun from my shoulder holster before I could fight back."

Webb flicked a match to life against the side of his desk and touched the flame to the point of his cigarette. The flame flared as Webb took a deep breath. "Before Child came to town, I wouldn't have questioned Ed Keller's word." He shook his head, then stared at the mine owner. "Get out, both of you. And if you kill each other, do it outside of town and my jurisdiction."

Keller cursed the marshal. "You turning coward, Webb? Afraid to do your job and arrest this man for murdering Van Mc-Cracken, who was nothing but a harmless old drunk?"

"My job," answered Webb, his anger rising, "is to enforce the law, which isn't the same thing as following your orders." The marshal pointed his cigarette at Keller. "By the way, why was McCracken carrying a sawed-off shotgun with your initials engraved in the stock?"

The mine owner's eyes and mouth widened and his face paled.

Webb grabbed a ring of keys from his desk and stepped to the nearby gun cabinet. He unlocked the door and reached inside. His hand emerged with the weapon that Van McCracken had carried when he died. "Isn't this the shotgun you've been known to hide under your coat when you carry sizable amounts of money?"

Keller shook his head, then took the

shotgun from the sheriff. He studied the weapon and ran his fingers over his initials in the stock.

Virgil thought Keller was stalling to think up an excuse.

"It looks like mine," he admitted, "but I haven't used it in a while. Somebody must have stolen it."

The marshal took the weapon back. "Sure, Mr. Keller. They didn't steal it off of you or you'd come running to me. If they'd broke into your place, I'd heard about it. It just don't make sense."

Keller licked his lips, then pointed at Virgil. "It's him. He's been sweet-talking Priscilla. I figure he convinced her to slip out with the shotgun for him."

Virgil felt his fists knotting. How could a man drag his own daughter down just to try and save his own worthless hide? "Liar," he said, spitting the word out like bile.

Keller ignored Virgil and kept on talking, almost pleading with the marshal. "Then he got McCracken to come to his room so he could kill him and make it look like I had something to do with his murder."

Shaking his head, Webb turned and slipped the shotgun back in the gun cabinet and locked it up. The marshal twisted around and stared at Keller. "Get out, Mr.

Keller. Your money can do a lot, but it can't turn a lie into the truth."

Keller shook his fist at Webb. "You won't be marshal of this town by the time I get through with you."

Webb shrugged. "Get out, Ed."

Keller hesitated.

"Now," Webb demanded.

The mine owner stood stunned for an instant, then strode to the door, jerked it open and charged outside.

The marshal turned to Virgil. "I figure you're telling more of the truth than Keller, but it's still your word against his. Just a few days ago, I'd taken his word for things, but not anymore, Virgil. You're like a demon from his past."

Virgil shook his head. "The demon is his conscience. I only awakened that demon."

"Maybe so, Virgil, but I'd watch my step if I were you. I still think we'd all be better off if you left."

"I'll be staying now until the dance is over, Marshal."

Webb nodded. "Then be careful. Keller could hire all sorts of men to kill you."

"Thanks, Marshal." Virgil marched out the door and headed back to the hotel.

Upstairs he found Ozanne cleaning up room number seven. He poked his head in

202

to say hello, but startled the proprietor.

"Oh," Ozanne said, "I thought you'd already gone into your room."

"Just got back from the marshal's office," he replied. "I'm planning on taking a little nap before lunch."

Ozanne nodded. "Good luck."

Virgil walked down the hall and shoved the key in the lock, but the door swung open at his touch. He figured he must've forgotten to lock it this morning when he left.

He stepped into the room, then caught his breath.

Standing in the corner was Tom Long, his gun drawn and pointed at Virgil's chest.

17

"Close the door nice and easy, son," ordered Tom Long, his voice soft but menacing. He waved his pistol at Virgil.

Virgil pushed the door shut, then gauged Long and whether he should try to defend himself. Virgil was as good as dead if he drew his pistol, because Long was sighted in on his heart.

"Now just so you don't get any ideas, unbuckle your gun belt, and let it slide to the floor."

Virgil hesitated.

Long cocked the hammer on his pistol. "If my finger so much as flinches, you're a dead man, like your father."

Slowly, Virgil lifted his hands to his waist. After unhooking the buckle, he let one end of the gun belt fall to the floor, then dropped the other end.

Grinning, Long released the hammer on his pistol and reholstered it.

Long pointed to the room's far corner. "Move over there, away from your gun."

Virgil obliged.

"I hear you killed Van McCracken this morning."

Virgil nodded.

"Good for you. He was nothing but a drunk. Keller bought him out for years with a few bottles of whiskey. Damn shame, too, when Van could've gotten so much more from Keller."

"What do you want, Long?"

Long laughed. "I want to kill you."

Virgil eyed his gun on the floor, wondering whether or not to make a play for it.

Long seemed to read his mind. "Not today, though, unless you try something stupid like going for your gun. Day after tomorrow. That's when I plan to kill you."

"Why the wait?"

"You see, son —"

"Don't call me 'son' again," Virgil growled. "That privilege belongs to the man you killed."

Long lifted his finger to his hat and flicked the brim. "Makes no difference to me. Now as to your question, I'm waiting so I can get both you and Ed Keller out in the malpais. That's where I'll kill you. The law'll never find us there, and when I'm done I can hide your bodies so God Himself couldn't find you with a map."

Virgil replied, "Keller and I aren't on the best of terms. No way we'll ride out for you."

Long's narrow lips curved into a sinister smile. "I figure I'll find a way to get you two to come after me."

"You're crazier than a mustang on locoweed. Why've you decided to kill Keller?"

Rubbing the stubble on his whiskered chin, Long cocked his head. "You see, before you showed up, the threat that you might one day return like your momma promised kept him nervous all these years. And, after he turned respectable, he feared word would get out about how he came to own the Deadman claim. That's why I was able to squeeze money out of him."

Virgil nodded.

"Now that you finally showed up, his fear has a face to it. Scared as he might be, he still believes he can kill you or have someone do it for him. Once you're dead, he's nothing to fear from you, and less to fear about me bringing up past history that no one but him and me can verify."

Long laughed. "The way I see it, if he dies, you'll still come after me. If you die, he tries to cut me off again. He tried that once before, about two years ago. Worst mistake he ever made, because his wife died." Long laughed. "Bless her heart, she was a fine woman, well liked by everyone, and nearly every man, woman and child from these parts attended the funeral. But I was the only one there that knew what killed her."

Virgil caught his breath and gritted his teeth for a moment. He lifted his finger and pointed it at Long. "You killed her?"

Long grinned. "Keller was getting slow about paying me what I demanded. Cyanide's easy to find in a mining town."

"You poisoned her, you son of a bitch?"

Long accentuated his nod with a laugh.

"No one knew how she died?"

Again, Long laughed. "I figure the doctor and the undertaker had suspicions, but they didn't say much about it, probably fearing that Keller had poisoned her. After his wife died, Keller started meeting my demands again. Of course, I had to remind him what a shame it would be if Priscilla were to die as suddenly as her mother."

Virgil's hands knotted into fists and he made a move for the opposite side of the corner, but before he could take two steps, Long had jerked and cocked his revolver.

"I wouldn't try anything."

Virgil backed away.

"That's better." Long lowered his pistol and slipped it back in its holster. "Day after tomorrow, come to the malpais, where I'll be waiting. Both of you better come together."

"Or what?"

Long grinned and flicked the brim of his hat. "Just do what I say." He spun around for the door and was outside in the hallway before Virgil could react.

Virgil stood in the corner, trying to sort out all that Long had revealed. The man must be insane if everything he had said was true. There was no way Virgil would accompany Ed Keller to the malpais. Was this just an insidious trick that Long had contrived with Keller? What could Virgil do, where could he turn?

There was Priscilla, but she was a young woman, not much more than a few years removed from pigtails, or from her mother's death! The thought that Long poisoned her mother turned his stomach.

Virgil retrieved his gun belt, strapped it around his waist, then shook his head. He had someone to see. He emerged from his room and strode down the hallway, down the stairs and out the front door, headed for Weatherby's Funeral Parlor.

The bell hanging over the door tinkled as

Virgil went inside. He found Tyrone Weatherby in the back room, bent over a cheap coffin.

Weatherby turned around and nodded. "I was just finishing up McCracken."

Virgil grimaced. He'd never killed a man before. And even if it was self-defense, a decent man couldn't help but have a tinge of remorse.

"You hit him square in the heart," Weatherby added. "That's steady shooting against a man with a sawed-off shotgun."

Virgil didn't know what to say. He hadn't planned on viewing McCracken's body. He just had to know if it was a possibility that Priscilla's mother had been poisoned.

"Funny thing about McCracken," Weatherby said. "I've seen him almost daily about town for the seven years I've been in White Oaks. Not once in all that time did I ever see him smile. But when I picked him up and brought him over, there was a smile on his face, as if he'd finally found peace with himself, instead of the bottle."

"I wouldn't know."

Weatherby nodded. "Undertakers look for things like that. It's not that we're morbid, just that we try to find something uplifting about what we do."

"I thought the money did that."

209

Weatherby grinned. "It helps, but we've still got to live with ourselves. Give me a minute and I'll cover him up. I can tell you're a bit uncomfortable around a dead man."

The undertaker folded McCracken's hands over his waist, straightened his collar, then pulled the wooden top over the coffin. He turned around. "If you came to check on the stone for your mother and father, it'll be a couple more weeks at the earliest."

"I came to talk about the death of Priscilla Keller's mother."

Weatherby's eyes narrowed and he answered with a slight nod.

"Anything unusual about it?"

"Why are you asking this?" Weatherby wanted to know.

Virgil studied the undertaker. "Was she murdered?"

Weatherby's shoulders sagged and he looked behind Virgil as if to see if anyone might be listening. "You're gonna try to say Keller murdered her like the rumors going around that he murdered your father."

"No," Virgil answered. "This isn't about Keller. There's another possibility."

Weatherby's eyes widened. "Keller's never been an easy man, but I didn't figure him to be so hard as to kill his wife. Still, that

210

was a possibility me and the doctor discussed. We never discussed it with anyone else, not even the marshal. Keller being a powerful man, we were afraid of him.

"Constance Keller, or Connie as most folks called her, was as decent as the Bible and as friendly as a stray puppy. Everybody liked her, and she made Keller a better man. Once she died, though, the hard edge returned that some of the old-timers used to speak of when he was younger. I couldn't believe he would kill her."

Virgil nodded. "Was it cyanide?"

Weatherby grimaced, then nodded slowly, deliberately. "That's what I think it was. When I was embalming her, I smelled a bitter almond odor about her body. It's one of the things undertakers pick up."

"So?"

"The almond odor is a sign of cyanide poisoning. I figure she was poisoned. Before she died, Connie fell dizzy, started vomiting and had convulsions — all indicators of cyanide poisoning."

"Why didn't you tell anyone?"

Weatherby sighed. "Ed Keller ran this town with his money and his clout. He was the only person we thought it could've been, because everybody else cared for Connie, her being as decent a sort as she was. Too,

211

we had no proof. Marshal Webb's one that demands ironclad proof before he gets serious with taking a man to trial. I don't know if he ever suspected Connie's death as anything other than an unexplained tragedy."

"Thanks for leveling with me, Weatherby." The undertaker smiled. "Now, you level with me. Who was it that poisoned her?"

Virgil studied Weatherby a moment. "It might be best I didn't tell you, Wetherby. The man that did it is as mean as they come and wouldn't hesitate to kill you."

"Tom Long, isn't it."

Taken by surprise, Virgil nodded before he realized he had given away the killer's identity.

"After I thought about it, Long's the only one around that would be mean enough to harm a woman as precious as Connie Keller. Damn him to hell. There's always been bad blood between him and Keller."

Virgil patted Weatherby on the shoulder. "Keep it quiet or you could be in danger."

"But how did you find out?"

"Long himself told me. He's trying to draw me out of town so he can kill me."

"He's a snake if I ever saw one. It'd be a pleasure to bury him."

"Thanks, Weatherby," Virgil said. "When

the time's right, I'll tell the marshal. Until then, keep it quiet."

The undertaker nodded as he escorted Virgil to the door. "You be careful, Virgil. Tom Long's not one to be trifled with."

The bell on the door tinkled as Weatherby shut it behind Virgil. Virgil toyed with the idea of visiting the marshal. but there was no proof, just talk. As sure as Virgil went to Webb, word would get out about his accusations, complicating his situation even more.

Weatherby had verified what Virgil had seen: The marshal didn't make a move until he was certain he had the right man. This would be Virgil's word against that of another man. He cursed his luck and started back to the hotel, then changed direction and went toward Reed's Mercantile.

At the store, he recognized the clerk who had sold him the clothes for his mother's funeral. The clerk greeted him. "Something about you must've driven McCracken loco, him coming after you with a shotgun. Any idea what it was?"

Virgil shook his head. He didn't care to discuss the killing. "I need six boxes of bullets for my pistol."

The clerk nodded. "That's forty-five ammunition, isn't it?"

"Yes, and do you have any good rifles

that'll shoot forty-fives?"

"I've got a Winchester carbine Model 1886 we took on trade. It's in good shape and shoots forty-five-seventy ammunition."

"How much?"

"Twenty-five dollars."

"Throw in a saddle scabbard for it and I'll take it."

The clerk scratched his head, then nodded. "Going hunting, are you?"

"You might put it that way," he answered.

After settling with the clerk, Virgil returned to the hotel.

From the front desk, Ozanne eyed Virgil, taking in his new carbine and the extra ammunition.

"I need you to do something for me," Virgil told the proprietor. "Can you deliver a note to Priscilla Keller?"

Ozanne nodded. "I can see that it gets there."

Virgil sat his carbine and cartridges on the counter, then took a piece of paper and wrote her a message. He folded it and put it in the envelope Ozanne provided.

Taking the envelope, Ozanne said, "It'll be there within the next thirty minutes."

"Put it in her hand," commanded Virgil, "and no one else's."

214

18

Priscilla Keller walked into the hotel after dark, just as Virgil Child had requested in his note. Sitting in a corner chair awaiting her, Virgil jumped up as soon as she entered. He strode across the room, grabbed her arm, turned her around and headed back outside.

"What's the matter?" she asked.

He shook his head and directed her down the street and toward the edge of town where they could talk without being seen or overheard.

"Where are we going?" she whispered.

He heard fear in her question. "Not far, just away from folks."

"Why?"

"Less likely we'll be seen there."

"Is it about Van McCracken?" she asked, her breath heaving.

Virgil was walking so fast, he realized Priscilla was virtually running to keep up. He slowed his pace, but said nothing more until they passed the final building with lit lamps.

"Is it something I've done?"

"No, no," Virgil answered, stopping and pulling her into his arms. He could feel the warmth of her breath against his shirt and could smell the fragrance of her hair.

"Father told me this afternoon that McCracken had stolen his shotgun and used it to try to kill you. He said you'd try to blame him for that, that you'd already accused him of giving the shotgun to McCracken with instructions to kill you."

Virgil said nothing. To speak would be to accuse Priscilla's father of just that and more.

"Father's not perfect, but he's not that mean, either."

Virgil cleared his throat. "I don't know your father, Priscilla, but I do know there are some men in his past that he's had reason to fear because of what they knew."

"Who?"

"Van McCracken and Tom Long."

"He never feared them. He tried to help McCracken. Long's a mean one, who Father tried to steer clear of. Why could he possibly fear them?"

Virgil wondered if he should tell her what he knew. He knew she would not betray his trust, but would she turn against him? He feared that.

"Did your father ever tell you he was once partners with McCracken and Long?"

"Father never talked much about business, but he wouldn't be partners with a drunk and a man like Long."

Virgil sighed. "Are you sure you want to know all this? I can't prove it all, but here's what I put together from what Momma said before she died plus what Jack Parmaley and Tom Long told me."

"You spoke to Tom Long?"

"Twice."

"I wouldn't believe a thing he said."

"Maybe not," Virgil said, "but his pieces of the puzzle fit together."

"Remember it's my father you're talking about."

Virgil let out a deep breath and shook his head. "I know, Priscilla, I know." He looked down at her face, but he could not really make out her expression, not in the darkness. "Some years ago, your father, along with McCracken and Long, found sign of gold in what is now Keller Gulch. The land was claimed by my father, who didn't know of the gold. They wanted the land, but he wouldn't give it up, so they shot him in front of my momma."

Priscilla pushed herself away. "Father wouldn't do that."

"Even if he didn't, Priscilla, he wound up with the claim and built the Deadman Mine, eventually taking over McCracken's and Long's shares before the mine hit big money.

"The two of them were bitter when the mine turned up so much gold, and they clung to your father like leeches. Mc-Cracken was easy to disarm because he liked to drink and your father kept him supplied in liquor, always paying his account for whiskey at Reed's Mercantile. Long, though, was shrewder. Whenever he needed money, he'd always threaten to reveal your father's part in my father's murder. Your father'd pay him to keep quiet."

"Who told you this?"

"Tom Long himself. And that's not all he told me. Priscilla, this is where it gets hard."

"How can it be any harder than telling me my father's a murderer and a thief?"

Virgil shook his head, knowing he should never have opened the subject up. "Maybe we should head back."

"No, I want to know the story, all of it."

Virgil took a couple deep breaths.

"Go on," Priscilla pleaded. "This can't be any worse."

Virgil pulled her closer to him. "But it is."

"Please tell me."

Running his fingers through her red hair, he spoke, his voice coming out as little more than a whisper. "A couple years ago, your father told Long he wasn't paying him any more." Virgil felt her nod her head against his chest.

"I remember right before Mother died that Father and Long had an argument in his office. He visited the house once more. I remember it, because it was the day Mother died. Father was at the mine and Mother and I were home alone. He visited with Mother a few minutes, brought her some wild plums. Father and I never liked plums, but they were Mother's favorites. Not long after he left, Mother took ill." Priscilla began to sniffle.

Virgil stroked her hair. "Long's visit wasn't a coincidence."

"What!" Priscilla pulled away from Virgil. "What do you mean?"

"He poisoned her."

"No," Priscilla cried, "don't tell me that."

"Long told me he used cyanide. Must've been in the plums."

Priscilla began to sob. "It's not true, please don't let it be true."

"I didn't believe it, Priscilla, but I went to

Tyrone Weatherby and asked. He said he thought she had been poisoned and the doctor thought so, too, but they didn't know a soul in town who didn't love your mother, and they didn't believe your father would do it."

"Why'd Long tell you this?"

"He's threatened to kill me and your father in the malpais day after tomorrow. Said he'd expect both of us to ride together for him. He's crazy. There's no way your father and I'd ride together after him."

Priscilla dabbed at her tears. "Why haven't you told the marshal?"

"There's nothing the marshal can do. Long'd just say I'm making up as many things about him as your father's accused me of making up about him. A court could never convict him." Virgil drew her back to him, but she started sobbing and hitting his chest.

"No, no, why did it have to be Mother?"

Virgil grabbed her hands and held them, hoping that she was frustrated by the truth rather than by him.

"I think I need to go home now," she managed between sobs. "I've got too many things to think over, and too many questions to ask Father."

"Certainly," Virgil replied. "Whatever you

wish." He turned her toward the lights of White Oaks and slipped his arm in hers. They walked slowly, neither of them saying a thing. Besides their footfalls on the rocky soil, Priscilla's whimpering was the only sound between them.

By the time they reached the first lit building, she had managed to control her emotions.

Virgil wondered if he had done the right thing by her. Maybe it was best sometimes just to leave the truth unsaid. He didn't know what was best. He did know that he'd never felt more helpless than when she was crying. It seemed nothing he could do would stop her tears or take back her hurt.

He squeezed her arm gently. "Let me see you home," he offered.

"No," she whispered. "I need to think things through and have a talk with Father. It would anger him to see me with you."

"I'd feel better walking you to your gate, even trailing behind you, just to know you got home safely."

"No!" She spoke emphatically, and Virgil could not tell if it was anger or exasperation. Or hate.

He leaned toward her and kissed her on the hair, relishing its softness and her womanly fragrance.

She did not respond to his kiss, but neither did she seem angered by it. When they reached a cross street, she pulled her arm softly from his. "It's shorter if I turn here rather than at the hotel," she said as she stepped away from him.

"Good night," he called softly.

"Good night," she answered, "and do be careful. Don't let Tom Long hurt you."

Virgil watched her form disappear in the darkness, then he headed on to the hotel. Ozanne was sweeping the floor when Virgil walked by the desk. "Good night," the proprietor called, but Virgil only nodded.

He walked by number seven and saw a temporary wooden patch on the door, then moved to his new room. He undressed in the dark, hanging his gun belt over the bedpost by his head.

After turning the covers, he fell onto the mattress, wondering what Priscilla was thinking, questioning whether he had done the right thing by her and wondering whether she planned to talk to her father before she retired for the night.

So much had happened since his mother's death that Virgil wasn't sure he had figured it all out or put together all the pieces of his life. He wondered what course his life might have taken had his father never been murdered. Would he have been rich? Would his mother still be alive? Would he be married? He didn't know, though he admitted he had never met another woman who had intrigued him as much as Priscilla Keller.

He wanted to court her, but how could she agree to go with a man who had considered killing her father? Then again, surely she could understand Virgil's grief, having lost her mother to a murderer like Tom Long.

Virgil gritted his teeth at the thought of Tom Long. He was a despicable man. Virgil cursed the name of Tom Long. Long was as vicious a man as Virgil had ever seen. He seemed to relish the misery he handed others. Long was so evil that Virgil could almost feel sorry for Ed Keller for ever hooking up with him.

And, Long was certainly insane to think that Virgil and Keller would ride into the malpais so he could settle a debt with them. That was as foolish as caging dogs with cats.

After a couple hours of so many questions and so few answers, Virgil fell to sleep. He awoke early, not on his own, but at a rapping on his door. He sat up and pulled his pistol from his holster. "Yes."

"Child, it's Marshal Webb. I need to talk to you."

"Go ahead," Virgil said, slipping his gun back in his holster.

"I think we better go to my office. I insist upon it."

"Trouble?" Virgil asked as he sat up, rubbed his eyes, then got up and began to dress.

"I've a couple questions I need to ask you. Ed Keller's been talking about you."

Virgil shook his head. Priscilla must've talked to her father last night. "I'll be right out."

"Fine," Webb said. "I'll be waiting downstairs."

After pulling his boots on, then wrapping his gun belt around him, Virgil headed out the door and down the stairs. Webb stood at the foot of the steps.

"What's this about?"

Webb pointed to the door. "We'll talk at my office. Some serious accusations have been made involving you."

As they reached the hotel door, Herb Ozanne barged out of the dining room behind them. "Mr. Child, Mr. Child . . . ," he started.

"Later," said Marshal Webb as he held open the door for Virgil.

Stepping out onto the street, Virgil turned toward the marshal's office.

224

"Were you out any last night after supper, Child?" the marshal asked, digging into his shirt pocket to start another cigarette.

"A while with Priscilla Keller."

Webb shook his head as he took a cigarette paper and filled it with pouch tobacco.

"There's no law against me seeing her."

"You know Ed Keller don't like her being out with you, not with all the accusations you've made against him," Webb said as he pulled the string on his tobacco pouch.

"Priscilla's old enough to decide who she wants to see and who she doesn't."

Webb nodded as he returned his tobacco pouch to his pocket. "Keller told me this morning he found your note asking her to meet you last night. Did you send her a note?"

"I did."

The marshal shoved the cigarette in his mouth, then fished a match out of his pocket and flicked it to life with the tip of his thumbnail.

"Why, Marshal?"

"You were the last person to see her last night. She never returned home."

19

Virgil Child felt his shoulders sag. He knew he should have accompanied her home last night. He'd gone against his instincts, and his instincts had been right. "No sign of her?"

Marshal Webb sucked deeply on his cigarette. "That's what we were hoping you would know."

"We?"

Webb nodded. "I've never seen Ed Keller as mad as he was when he came into the office. It took me a while to cool him off, but fact of the matter is, he's got a right to answers to his questions."

"I want answers just as much as Keller does. I've taken a liking to her."

Webb coughed a cloud of smoke. "If that don't beat all. You come to town with a grudge against a fellow and then take a fancy to his daughter. You sure this isn't just some ploy of yours to drag Keller into a fight?"

"I came here looking for a grave, not a fight."

"You may find your own grave before this plays out," Webb said.

Striding in step, the two men turned the corner and aimed for the marshal's office. Webb's jaw was set and his gaze was fixed on Virgil. "There's been nothing but trouble since you came to town. When are you getting out? I want an answer."

"I came to White Oaks looking for a few answers myself. Seems my questions made a few folks uncomfortable. Keller himself offered me ten thousand dollars just to leave. I refused his offer, and I'll refuse all others until I get answers. Then I'll leave town, but not before."

Webb said nothing, just took several deep drags on his smoke until he neared his office. Then he removed the nub of his cigarette and flicked it into the middle of the street, where it smoldered.

"Am I under arrest?" Virgil asked.

"You still got your gun, don't you?"

Virgil nodded.

"Then you're not under arrest. There's just some questions I want answered. Questions I want answered in front of Keller.

Between the two of you, I don't know who to trust anymore."

Virgil loosed a sarcastic laugh. "I thought Keller was White Oaks' most respected citizen."

Webb grabbed Virgil's arm and stopped him in the street in front of the jail. "He's the richest for sure. A week ago I might've said the most respected, but some things don't add up, like his shotgun winding up in Van McCracken's hands. McCracken was a drunk who might've stolen a drink or money to buy a drink, but never a shotgun like Keller said."

Releasing Virgil's arm, Webb pointed to the jail. "Keller's in there waiting. He's got a right to be riled because his girl's missing, but don't you make things any worse."

When they reached the jail door, Webb held it open for Virgil to enter ahead of him. As Virgil walked in, he saw Keller jump up from a chair and charge across the room.

"Where is she, you son of a bitch, where is she?" he yelled, his hands outstretched as if he planned to strangle Virgil.

Instinctively, Virgil's hand fell to the gun at his side, but Webb grabbed Virgil's wrist and stepped between him and Keller.

Keller barged into Webb, but the marshal stuck up his hand and shoved Keller back.

"Watch what you're doing," Keller yelled. "You're not just pushing another drunk about, Webb."

The marshal released Virgil's hand and spun about to face Keller. "And you're not pushing the law around, Keller."

"Don't think you're the law, Webb, because I can have you replaced real quick."

"Until then," Webb said, his voice menacingly low, "I'm the law, and you'll respect that or you'll be behind bars for a while."

Keller lifted his finger and pointed it at Virgil. "He's the one that needs to be behind bars. Where's my girl?"

Webb pointed to a chair on the opposite side of the room. "Sit down, Keller, and this'll go a lot faster."

The mine owner grumbled indecipherably and backed to the chair, but remained standing.

The marshal motioned for Virgil to sit on the bench in front of his desk. Virgil took his seat.

Grumbling under his breath, Keller cocked his head at the marshal.

Webb crossed his arms over his chest and stared back at Keller. "When you sit down, we'll try to get to the bottom of this."

Keller stood defiant for a moment, but could not stare the badge down. Angrily, he plopped in the chair.

The marshal nodded at him. "I want to hear what both of you have to say about this. I don't know that I believe either one of you. Go ahead, Keller, now tell me everything."

"I told you once," Keller grumbled.

"Tell me again, in front of Virgil here."

Keller's face reddened in anger and he pointed at Virgil. "He's the one you should be questioning, not me."

"Do as I say, Keller."

Reaching in his shirt pocket, Keller grumbled, "When my housekeeper went to wake Prissy for breakfast this morning, she found her room empty and her bed unturned. She notified me and I looked around and couldn't find her, but I did come across this." He pulled a note from his pocket and waved it at Virgil. "The note said for her to meet him at the hotel last night, just after full dark."

Crossing the room, Webb took the note and started toward Virgil. "Did you write this?"

"You don't need to show me," Virgil admitted, "because I wrote it. Ozanne saw that it was delivered for me."

"Why didn't you take it yourself?" the marshal queried.

Virgil felt his jaw clench for a moment. He pointed at Keller. "You think he'd welcome me in his house?"

"Hell, no," answered Keller, "not after you threatened me."

"Shut up, Keller," the marshal said to the mine owner, then turned to Virgil. "Why'd you want to see her?"

"I had things to discuss with her."

"Dammit, you wanted to hurt her," Keller said. "You've been stringing her along to get to me, haven't you?"

Marshal Webb jerked off his hat and flung it at Keller. "Shut up, for the last time."

Keller knocked the hat out of the air with his hand, then sat sullenly glaring at Virgil.

Webb turned back to Virgil and shook his head. "It doesn't wash that you had things to discuss with her, Virgil."

Virgil bit his lip. He didn't know how much to reveal or how much Webb might believe. So much of it sounded preposterous. But what choice did he have? Whether they believed him or not was not nearly so important now as finding Priscilla unharmed. He sighed.

"We're waiting, Virgil."

Virgil nodded. "Tom Long came to visit me after McCracken's death. He caught me by surprise in my room yesterday. He told

231

me a lot of things, things like Keller there paying him over the years to keep quiet about his involvement in my father's death."

"Liar," Keller said.

Virgil stared hard at Keller. "Two years ago you tried to cut him off, decided to quit paying him, didn't you?"

Webb looked at the mine owner and Keller shrugged, denying everything with his stone-faced demeanor.

"That's about the time your wife died, wasn't it?"

Keller's stone facade broke as his eyes widened and his face paled.

"After she died, he threatened to harm Priscilla if you didn't keep paying him. Didn't he?"

Keller bit his lip.

"That true?" asked Webb.

The mine owner nodded slightly.

"Long told me something else, something that was hard to believe. He said he had poisoned your wife. Said he used cyanide. Priscilla said Long had taken her mother some wild plums after a heated argument between the two of you."

Keller stood up from his chair and walked to the empty jail cell. His head sagged as he grabbed two of the bars and tried to shake them free of their hold. "No, dammit, no. I should've protected her from him. Why didn't I realize Tom Long would do that? He's the meanest man I was ever around."

Webb stroked his chin and shook his head. "Long admitted this to you."

"Yes, sir," Virgil said. "I know it's only my say so you've got to go on, but that's what he said. After I learned this, I wanted to talk with Priscilla, see if she remembered a visit from Long about the time her mother died. She did."

Keller began to sob. "Connie, Connie, why did I let this happen to you?"

Virgil continued. "I went to see Tyrone Weatherby. He told me when he laid out Constance Keller there was an almondlike aroma about her, the type of thing undertakers know as a sign of cyanide poisoning."

"The bastard," said Webb, shaking his head. "I'll have to check this out with Weatherby, of course." The marshal turned to Keller. "I'm sorry about Connie."

"I'll kill the bastard," Keller said, "if it takes every cent I've got."

Then it struck Virgil like a bolt of lightning. He shot up from his seat and hit his palm with his fist. "Damnation, I know where Priscilla is."

Keller spun around.

Webb cocked his head toward Virgil. "Go on."

"Long told me he planned to kill me and Keller. Told me yesterday he'd meet us in the malpais, day after tomorrow. I said he was crazy, that Keller and I would never ride together, even to kill such a sorry skunk as him."

"The son of a bitch," shouted Keller. "He took her."

"That's gotta be the answer," Webb interjected.

Virgil nodded. "I'm going for her."

"No, dammit, she's my daughter and I want the pleasure of killing him for what he did to Connie."

Webb shook his head. "The malpais is out of my jurisdiction, but from the way Keller tells it I won't be marshal much longer anyway. The three of us'll go after him. I don't want you two killing each other once you get him."

Virgil started for the door. "I need to get my carbine and ammunition from the hotel."

"I want to check with Weatherby about Connie," Webb said. "Not that I don't trust you, Virgil, but I just gotta hear it for myself. Keller, you buy a couple days' supplies from Reed's Mercantile and get an extra canteen apiece. Let's meet in half an hour at the livery stable."

The three men nodded and headed out the door, each going his separate way, but all aimed at the same ultimate destination. Virgil fairly ran to the hotel, barging in and dashing for the stairs. Behind him he heard Ozanne yelling.

"Mr. Child, Mr. Child," he cried, "come back. I've an envelope for you, a message from Tom Long."

Virgil froze in his tracks for a moment, the rage building in him. He spun around and bolted back down the steps and over to the desk. He jerked the envelope from Ozanne's hand and ripped the flap off. His heart was pounding as he unfolded the paper and began to read the scrawled handwriting.

"I've got the girl. I'll trade her life for yours and Ed's in the malpais tomorrow. Just you and Ed should come. If I see more than two riders, I'll kill her. Tom Long."

Virgil cursed.

"Bad news?" Ozanne asked.

Virgil spun around and ran up the stairs to his room, shoving the note in his vest pocket. He grabbed his new carbine in its saddle boot, then jerked the case off his pillow and used it as a bag to carry the new boxes of ammunition. He darted downstairs, not taking time to even shut his door.

The bewildered Ozanne stared, then yelled as he ran out the door, "Where are you going with my pillowcase?"

Without answering, Virgil dashed down the street, then turned toward the livery stable. He was the first to reach the stable and he darted inside, ignoring the liveryman and finding the first stall with one of his mules. He slipped the bridle over the mule's head, then saddled the animal, snagged his saddle scabbard to the rigging and tied the pillowcase of ammunition to the saddle horn.

He led the animal outside to a water trough and gave it a chance to drink its fill before starting for the malpais.

After what seemed like an eternity, Virgil spotted the marshal running toward him. Webb nodded as he approached out of breath. "Weatherby confirmed what you said, Virgil."

Virgil dug into his vest pocket and retrieved the note, dragging the bloody handkerchief out as well. "Tom Long left this for me."

Webb grabbed the note as Ed Keller approached, a burlap sack of supplies in each hand. As Webb read the note, he kept shaking his head. "The son of a bitch," he said.

Keller walked up, tossing Virgil a bag.

"We ain't got time for reading," Keller said.

"It's a note from Long," the marshal replied.

Keller jerked it from the marshal's hand. He read it quickly, let out a deep breath and looked at the marshal.

"Looks like you best stay, Marshal."

Webb bit his lip and and seemed to sag a bit.

Keller turned to Virgil. "I guess it's just you and me."

Virgil nodded.

Webb said, "You boys try to keep from killing each other."

20

Side by side they rode silently to the outskirts of White Oaks, Virgil Child on his mule and Ed Keller on a black gelding. Keller had offered to buy a horse for Virgil, but Virgil had declined. He knew the mule and knew the mule would get him to the malpais.

Virgil stared at the vast pile of gray tailings that covered his father's grave and shook his head. Had his father lived, Virgil wondered if the wealth extracted from that gravel would have made him the kind of man Keller was. Money had bought Keller whatever comforts he wanted, but it had not bought him a clear conscience — he seemed tormented by the deed which had brought him all that wealth. But at least Ed Keller had a conscience. Tom Long didn't. He was a reptile in the guise of a man.

Virgil would take pleasure in killing Long! He wasn't so certain about what he wanted to do with Ed Keller.

Virgil stared to the west as the midmorning sun at his back began to scorch the earth. He had expected it to be a hot day and a silent ride, but as the two men neared the road to the Deadman Mine, Keller surprised him with a question.

"Mind if I stop at the cemetery a minute?" His voice was remorseful, but calm. "There's some business I need to attend."

"It's tomorrow when Long said to meet him. You've plenty of time."

Virgil followed Keller's gelding off the road to the cemetery. As Keller dismounted, Virgil reached out to hold his reins. Keller bit his lip and handed the leather lines to Virgil.

Keller marched to the tall obelisk that was the headstone for Constance Keller. Virgil watched as the mine owner took off his hat and held it with both hands in front of his waist. Though Virgil could not tell for certain, he thought Keller was speaking to the monument. Time seemed to freeze as Keller lingered over his wife, shifting uncomfortably from foot to foot and rolling the brim of his hat between his fingers. When Keller turned around, he drew the sleeve of his shirt across his eyes, then pulled his hat over his head to hide them from Virgil.

As Keller approached, Virgil leaned over his saddle and extended the reins. The mine owner took them without looking up and quickly climbed into the saddle.

"She was a fine woman, Connie, better than I deserved," he said, then jerked the reins of the gelding and turned him toward the road.

Virgil nodded. "She must have been like Priscilla."

Keller said nothing, but rode at Virgil's side as they retreated to the Carrizozo road.

Straight ahead of them stood the mountain of tailings. Virgil could not pass up the chance to ask Keller the question he wanted confirmed. "Is my father buried there?"

Keller's head drooped a little more.

Virgil could not see the mine owner's eyes, but he could see him biting his lip. Then he noticed a nod so slight as to be almost imperceptible. Virgil didn't press him.

As they reached the road and turned toward Carrizozo, Virgil lifted his gaze from Keller and looked to the west toward the malpais. Finding Priscilla and rescuing her was more important at that moment than confirming what he already strongly suspected about his father's death.

Keller said nothing for a quarter mile,

then glanced over his shoulder at the mine works. "I'd trade it all," he said, "just to get Prissy back safe and to have Connie again."

Virgil took him as sincere.

"Your father's buried where you think he is," Keller continued. "His death made me a rich man. . . ."

Virgil shook his head. "You mean his murder?"

"Yes, dammit, his murder, if that's how you want it." Keller went silent and didn't say another thing for a mile or more.

Before them the distant heat shimmered in waves and the mountains beyond the malpais seemed to dance.

Keller let out a deep breath. "We were drunk when it happened." He bit his lip. "Gold. We'd found traces of gold on his place the day before. You know what it's like to know you are near a fortune?"

"Work's all I know."

Keller looked up at the scalded sky. "Gold. Why, you think it can solve all your problems. It just adds to them. I should know now after all these years. I thought I could buy you off whenever you showed up." Keller cursed. "But something good came out of you turning me down — I learned why Connie died, and I intend to kill that son of a bitch. He's lower than a snake's belly. The day we killed your father, he wanted to kill you and your mother while she's digging your father's grave. I've often wondered if I'd been less tormented had we gone ahead and done that, but I just couldn't kill a woman and child, even when I was drunk. Had Tom Long been sober, I'm not sure Van and I could've talked him out of it.

"I saw your mother in her coffin and she had a soft, kind look about her, much like Connie when I buried her, but you could tell by her hands that she'd done hard work."

"Why you telling me this now?"

"None of it seems important anymore; just getting Prissy back and destroying Tom Long is all that matters. Of course, that won't bring back Connie, or your folks."

Virgil took off his hat and drew the sleeve of his shirt across his sweaty forehead. "It's plenty hot, isn't it?"

Keller nodded. "Reminds me of the day we killed your father. We'd been drinking and celebrating our riches all night before we realized we might not be able to file a valid claim on the site. Maybe we'd thought straighter if we hadn't been drinking. I've always wondered if we'd been sober if one of us would've thought of working out a partnership with your father so we'd share the gold money. Then I remember that Tom Long was with us and he would've preferred killing him anyway. Fact is, I'm not sure why Tom didn't kill me and McCracken. Maybe he knew he didn't have what it took to run a mine.

"When the mine went down for a while, they lost faith, and both offered to sell me their shares for ten thousand dollars." He glanced at Virgil. "The same amount that I offered you to leave town. I had faith we'd bring the mine back up, so I bought them out. Then when I hit the main lode, they wanted back in, but I said no, they'd sold out and left me with all the risks. Then, both started reminding me that I was involved in your father's murder and they wanted a cut of my profits."

Though Keller's story didn't square entirely with McCracken's and Long's, Virgil saw no point in arguing.

"McCracken took to drink and was easy to keep drunk and satisfied, but Long, now he was greedy and kept threatening to tell everyone how we'd gotten the claim to begin with. By then, I'd married Connie and wanted a decent life for us. I sure didn't want her to know I'd killed a man in cold blood.

"After you get money, it does something

243

to you, makes you think you're something more than you really are. I know I'd kill to get money, because I've done it, but I don't know if I'd kill to keep from losing it, since it's cost me so much. Now, I've got a question for you, Virgil Child."

Virgil nodded. "Fair enough."

"You took to seeing Priscilla, even though I warned her against it. Were you just trying to find a way to get close enough to me to kill me?"

Virgil shook his head. "I didn't know all of these things when I came to White Oaks. I came to bury Momma, but when everyone starting trying to hide things from me about my father's death, I knew I had to find the answers. The more you hid and the more I found out, the more I considered killing you."

Keller stroked his chin. "You still planning on killing me?"

After a pause, Virgil shrugged. "I don't know and won't know until after we save Priscilla. What about you?"

"Like I said, I don't know if I'd kill to keep money or not."

The two men stared each other in the eye. An understanding had passed between them. First they would find Priscilla and kill Tom Long. Then they would decide what to do with each other. They rode wordlessly for two more hours, bound to get her by the tenuous threads of a murder almost two decades past and a woman, little more than a girl, in danger.

They took occasional drinks from their canteens, but didn't pause for a bite of lunch, riding until early afternoon, when they reached the edge of the malpais. Virgil had never seen such rugged ground. In some places it was black and pitted like a great sponge turned to stone; in others, the basalt had hardened into perpetual stone waves. To the northwest Virgil saw a cone-shaped black peak that had hundreds of years before spewed the molten rock and then died after scarring the earth. The day was hot, but even hotter over the black rock, which seemed to hold the heat.

Virgil did not relish riding out onto the malpais. The heat would sap his energy; the sharp rocks would cut the mule's hooves and his own boots if he went afoot. But as hard as it might be for him, Virgil figured it must be harder for Priscilla Keller, out there somewhere in the malpais, perhaps hidden in some wide crevice or bubble cave made by the lava centuries before.

Keller broke the silence. "It's six miles wide at its widest, but forty-four miles long." He pointed back south toward Carrizozo. "There's maybe a third of it running southwest of town. The rest and the widest parts are to the north."

"Which way you think he'd go?" Virgil asked.

"A sane man'd stay closer to town for the water, but Long's too mean to be sane. I figure he went north. More places to hide, and farther away from the law."

"Can mounts make it over the top?" Virgil asked.

"They'll get cut up pretty bad, but they're only animals."

Virgil nodded. "And we don't have any choice."

Keller pointed at the burlap sack hanging over his saddle horn. "There's some tins of tomatoes and peaches if you want a bite."

"I'm not hungry. Let's save it for later."

"Suit yourself."

Virgil nudged his mule ahead. The animal stepped tentatively upon the black rock and tossed his head. "Easy, fellow," Virgil said. "Take your time and get used to it. We've a lot of looking to do before we return to White Oaks."

Keller's mount balked at advancing onto the rocks, but Keller slapped his reins against the animal's neck and the stallion lunged forward, stumbling on the awkward footing.

Virgil steered his mule between dangerous crevices and razor-sharp lava prongs. He rode the mule some fifty yards into the malpais, then dismounted.

"I can either look for Priscilla or watch my mule's footing," he told Keller, "but not both."

Keller dismounted and wrapped his reins around his wrist. "We need to spread out, put maybe a quarter of a mile between us, and start working our way north."

"Let's stay in view of each other. He'll see us before we see him. Maybe we can get the drop on him, but let's not try to down him until we're sure where Priscilla is."

Keller nodded. "Let's get going."

The two men began to weave their way through the rugged terrain, leading their mounts behind them. Quickly the heat of the malpais began to soak through the soles of Virgil's boots, and his feet seemed to roast in the leather oven. The sun burned so hot that it seemed as if Virgil were carrying it on his shoulder and as if his skin were frying beneath his shirt.

Despite the rugged basalt, cacti had taken root in crevices and intermittent patches of soil, increasing the dangers to passing man

and animal. In trying to avoid the dangerous rocks, Virgil occasionally brushed
against one of the bushes, cursing at the
pain, then stopping to pull a thorn from his
britches or his flesh.

He surveyed the land before him, taking
in the full sweep of the ugly terrain. All he
saw was black rock, prickly ocotillo and
cholla and an occasional rodent scurrying
into a hole. Overhead, a hawk with wings
extended circled the molten sky on the
invisible wind currents.

Virgil saw nothing except Keller out of
the corner of his eye. Soon his shirt was as
wet with perspiration as his throat was dry.
He pushed himself until he could wait no
longer, then stopped the mule and took a
sip from his canteen. Then he went on, his
progress as slow as the passing of time on
this godforsaken patch of earth.

He kept walking, but the heat was sapping
him. He kept looking, but the emptiness
was frustrating him. He kept cursing to
himself, for the mere sound of his own
voice. He kept wishing he had accompanied
Priscilla home that night and had had the
chance to kill Tom Long.

Virgil was surprised when the sun finally
slipped behind the mountains to the west.
The shade brought relief, and he took off

his hat and began to fan his face. He was hungry, thirsty and tired. He was mad, frustrated and vengeful. He kept walking, gradually angling back toward Keller, who was a bit slower.

When he came within talking distance of the mine owner, he saw the shared frustration. They said nothing, just kept moving ahead until it was too dark to move safely over the rugged terrain.

"I'm ready for a can of those peaches," Virgil said, surprised at the coarseness of his voice. "We can't go any farther in the dark."

"Not one damn sign of them," Keller said.

They hobbled their horses and opened tins of peaches for supper. The basalt was still hot, so they stood or walked carefully around until the ground cooled off enough to throw bedrolls. They had nothing more to say to each other, and didn't even try.

They were making their bedrolls when they heard a gunshot from the north. They looked toward the black peak in the distance and saw a spark of fire from a second gunshot, the sound reaching them a moment later. Then they saw another spark, lower to the ground, that gradually became a fire.

"That's bound to be him," Keller said.

"No other fool would be out here in the middle of the malpais."

Virgil nodded. "But what's he burning? No wood about?"

"Likely cactus stalks. Think we should try for him in the dark?"

"No," Virgil replied. "We'd be just like moths to a flame. He'd see us and shoot us down."

"He can see us come morning."

"That's right," Virgil said, "but we'll have a better chance of seeing him and finding Priscilla. That's just as important."

Virgil drew his pistol and held it in the air. He snapped off two quick shots.

"What's that for, dammit?"

"To let Priscilla know that we're near."

"Come morning, we'll be even nearer," Keller said.

21

After an uneasy night of worry, Virgil Child and Ed Keller were up an hour before dawn, saddling their mounts and checking the load of their weapons. Virgil Child, thirsty and edgy, glanced several times toward the mountains to the east to gauge the approach of dawn.

In those mountains this whole drama had begun some twenty years ago. Where White Oaks now stood there had once been a rancher with wife and child. And there had been gold which made the mountain valuable. Now the rancher was dead, but his boy had grown up and returned. The killings that had started over valuable land would now be resolved by death on a worthless stretch of New Mexico Territory.

Only the darkness could hide the land's ugliness. It looked like frozen hell and was almost as dangerous. Virgil dreaded the dawn, not just because he feared for Priscilla's life, but also because he didn't care to look at this ugly landscape anymore.

Virgil pulled his carbine from its saddle scabbard. He could just make out Keller as a shadowy form ten paces away. Though he wasn't worried about Keller for the time being, once they rescued Priscilla and killed Tom Long, Virgil doubted he could trust Keller on the return to White Oaks. But that worry could come later; his first concern was saving Priscilla. He turned toward Keller. "I figure we should try to get as close as we can before good light."

"That means leaving the mounts behind," Keller said.

"We can travel faster afoot than mounted, and there's less chance he would see us."

"Suits me," Keller replied. "I just want to get Long before he knows what hit him."

Virgil took a deep breath. "Long wouldn't have done anything to Priscilla, do you think?"

Keller remained silent for a moment. "Long's too mean for that. He'd wait until we could see him kill her."

Virgil cursed. "The bastard." He paused a moment, then asked a question that would be important to have answered before the showdown with Long. And, afterward as well. "How many weapons are you carrying on you?"

"My carbine and sidearm."

"No hidden pistol?"

"Not since you took it. What about you?"

"Same as you," Virgil said, patting the carbine cradled in his arm. "We best get moving. Let's try to stay about fifty yards apart. And be careful — we don't want to do anything that might endanger Priscilla."

"Understood."

As one, they moved forward, Virgil angling away from Keller and aiming for the spot where he had seen the fire last night. In the dark, it was difficult to be certain he was headed for the appropriate place. He crouched low over the ground and took short steps to keep from cutting himself on the sharp rocks or sticking himself on the cacti.

He brushed up against a cholla and felt a thorn pierce his britches and stick his leg. As he reached for the thorn, he heard a buzzing sound at his feet and froze.

Rattlesnake!

Virgil held his breath and the buzzing softened. Easily, Virgil backtracked until the buzzing died. He paused to jerk the thorn from his leg, then circled wide of the spot where he had heard the rattler.

Glancing to the east, he saw the sky paling pink above the mountaintops. It was still too dark for him to see Keller, though occasionally he heard the mine owner curse at the hard going in the dark.

Virgil could see nothing for certain up ahead, just the odd shapes of the rocks and the scraggly bushes which had taken root in this petrified hell. In the darkness and over the rough terrain, he lost track of distance and grew confused about how close he might be to the site of the fire last night. He pondered his options and decided to advance until he found a good spot to hide. Maybe, just maybe, he would be in a position to spot Long and take a shot at him.

He inched ahead another fifteen minutes, then came to what seemed like a molten bubble in the black basalt. It would serve as a good vantage point.

Virgil squatted behind the rock and waited as the sky gradually began to lighten, slowly defining the land as more than just vague shapes. For half an hour, he saw nothing. Then to the east, he caught a brief glimpse of Keller, moving low to the ground. Keller seemed to have no more clue of his destination than Virgil.

Virgil twisted around, scanning the rugged black terrain from the west to the north and then to the east, where the sun was just clearing the Jicarilla Mountains around White Oaks.

The sun, already harsh, glared at the land, warning of another hot day ahead. Virgil cursed himself for not thinking to bring his canteen with him.

As his gaze retraced the terrain, he caught a sudden glint between a pair of black rocks. He squinted, trying to see what had caused the flash of light. He saw a length of steel he knew to be a rifle barrel. He lifted his carbine and took aim, but all he could see was the barrel, not who held the gun.

He was uncertain if Long was aiming at Keller or not. Virgil did not know whether to warn Keller and give away his position or to hope Long would miss. For all his differences with Keller, he could not let him die in an ambush.

"Long," Virgil yelled, "throw down your gun." Virgil saw the rifle barrel disappear behind the rock.

Long answered with a sinister laugh, followed by a scream. Priscilla's scream! It seemed to echo out of the ground, then roll over the hard landscape.

"You got it wrong, Child. You and Keller need to throw down your guns."

Virgil stared at Long's rocky fortress. It didn't make sense. He saw no horses. How had Long penetrated the malpais? Virgil knew he couldn't fly, but where were the horses?

"Throw down your guns," Long cried out again.

"Let the girl go," Virgil yelled.

Long laughed. "You fool. She's my bait. I'm not cutting her loose until you two are dead. And, maybe not then." He laughed again.

Keller yelled at Long. "You bastard, did you kill my Connie?"

"Where'd you hear something like that?"

"It don't matter, you bastard."

"Connie always did like wild plums," Long called out. "Yeah, I killed her, and if you don't give up, I'm gonna kill your daughter."

"Don't give up, just don't," cried Priscilla.

"Shut up, girl," cried Long.

Then came a gunshot and silence.

Virgil flinched, his mouth turning to cotton, and not from the heat.

"Prissy, Prissy," yelled a terrified Keller.

Virgil saw Keller stand up. Long laughed, then Priscilla called out.

"I'm fine. He just fired his gun and covered my mouth."

Long cursed, then issued another threat. "I'm gagging her. The next time I fire, you won't know whether I hit her or not." There was a long pause. "I'm counting to ten. If both of you haven't come on in carrying your rifles over your heads, I'm gonna kill her, or maybe not, only you won't know. One."

Virgil gritted his teeth.

"Two."

He felt his forehead beading with perspiration.

"Three."

"It's no use, Child," called Keller, "we've got to do what he says."

"Four," Long said, punctuating it with a shot from his rifle. "Just kidding," Long continued. "I didn't shoot her. Yet!"

Virgil began to rise.

"Five."

"Don't shoot," screamed Keller.

"Six."

"Do what he says," Keller pleaded, as he inched ahead, his hands over his head.

"Seven."

"I am," Virgil called back.

"Eight," Long yelled. "I can't see you, Child."

Virgil stood up and moved toward Long's position, holding his rifle over his head.

"Nine."

"We're both coming in," Keller cried in

desperation.

"Ten," Long shouted, then fired another shot and laughed. "Just riling you. I wouldn't kill her where you two couldn't see it."

Virgil and Keller advanced with their guns held over their heads, and Tom Long seemed to appear out of the ground. As Virgil neared Long's hiding place, he spotted the gray ash of the fire they had seen last night and the charred end of a cactus stalk that Long had used for fuel.

Tom Long waved them on in with his rifle, his smile as sinister as his intent. "You boys look a little worried. You ought to be." He licked his lips. "Hold your rifles by the barrel and put them down on the ground nice and easy."

Virgil watched Keller lower his weapon. Gritting his teeth, Virgil lowered his and dropped it on the petrified earth.

"Now," Long instructed, "with your left hands, pull your revolvers out of your holsters."

Both men obeyed.

"Child, I told you I'd get both of you to ride out here to meet your deaths." Then he looked at Keller. "You carrying one of them small guns under your coat or anything?"

Keller lifted the lapels of his coat so Long

could see he did not have an extra gun.

Long laughed. "What about the pea-shooter you used to carry in your boot?"

Keller grimaced, bent down and pulled a small revolver from top of his boot.

Virgil spat in disgust as Keller dropped the gun beside his rifle and pistol. Keller had lied to him about his weapons. Virgil knew for certain if he killed Long, he'd likely have to do the same with Keller.

Long swung his rifle back and forth at the chests of Virgil and Keller. Then he pointed to the twin rocks which had hidden him. "You boys come on over here."

Virgil started for the rocks, then stopped to allow Keller to pass in front of him. It was bad enough having one backshooter behind him; he didn't care for two.

Virgil followed Keller between the rocks, which screened a sloping passage some four feet wide.

Long followed them both. "Don't you boys make any sudden moves or I'll shoot you."

The stone path leveled out in a natural crevice some ten feet wide and thirty feet long. At one end Virgil saw two hobbled horses near a pool of water. At the other, he saw Priscilla Keller bound and gagged upon the ground. The side of her face was purple and bruised.

Virgil felt his fists tightening. He cursed as Long stabbed him in the back with the barrel of his rifle.

Virgil stumbled over a pile of dead cholla and ocotillo that Long had gathered to build fires.

"Move a little faster," Long commanded.

Keller jumped to his daughter and fumbled with the gag. "You okay?" he asked, cradling her against him as she spit out the wad of cloth.

Priscilla bit her lip and began to cry. She threw back her head and glared at Tom Long. "He's bruised me up a bit, but nothing that won't heal." She nodded toward the water. "I've had enough to drink and enough shade to survive."

Keller pulled his daughter to him, hugging her tightly.

"I hate him, Father, I hate him. He killed Mother, did you know that?"

Keller nodded. "I know now. Virgil told me. Long'll die for it, too."

Long laughed. "I ain't planning on committing suicide, Ed, so you got it all wrong. Fact is, I wouldn't bet on any of *you* seeing another sundown."

"Let the girl go, Long. That was part of the deal," Virgil demanded.

Long pointed the gun at Virgil's belly. "The deal was she'd live until I got you two here. You think I'd let her go now and run back to White Oaks telling everyone what I'd done?"

"What do you want, Long? I'll give it to you," Keller pleaded. "Want your share of the mine back? I'll sign the papers, whatever you want. Just let Prissy go."

Virgil knew time was running short. He had to do something, had to make some type of move if he ever wanted to see noon, much less sundown.

"Who wants to die first?" Long hissed. "I thought about the girl so you two fellas could see it, but then I might want to use her for a few things before I put her out of her misery. No, sir, I might save her for last. Then again, I might want to enjoy her while her pappy watches. Do to her what he did to me with the mine. Get even with you, Keller."

"You got even with me when you killed Connie, you son of a bitch."

Virgil edged toward the pile of dead cactus. He could never reach Long without being shot, but just maybe he could distract him with the cactus.

Long turned toward Virgil and grinned. "I guess I'll start with you, seeing as if I'd

261

killed you and your momma years ago we'd all been better off. Save you, of course." Long laughed as he raised his rifle to his shoulder.

22

Time seemed to freeze as the gun barrel aimed straight at Virgil's head. Long's hard gaze down the gun barrel locked on Virgil for an instant that seemed forever.

Virgil edged toward the pile of cactus stalks.

The gun barrel followed him.

Virgil gritted his teeth.

Long gave a final laugh.

Then, time raced by as Virgil dove for the butts of a pair of cactus stalks.

The gun exploded and the sound reverberated around the rock walls. Priscilla screamed. The horses by the water basin spooked and kicked against their hobbles. Long cursed his miss.

Virgil's bare hands circled the butt end of two stalks. He screamed as the thorns pricked his flesh. Virgil rolled away from the pile just as another bullet pinged off the ground where he had been.

Scrambling to his feet, Virgil drew back his right arm, screaming at the pain in his palm, but holding tight to the stalks as his only chance.

Long swung his rifle barrel in an arc that followed Virgil.

Virgil glimpsed a movement behind Long, then saw Ed Keller shove Long just as the rifle barrel spit flame.

The bullet scorched the air to Virgil's side.

Keller swatted at the rifle, but Long stumbled away from him, still within range of Virgil.

Virgil swung the cacti at Long's face.

One stalk hit Long full on the cheek. He lunged blindly forward. Virgil sidestepped him, then struck him with the second stalk against the side of the neck.

Blood ran down Long's face from several punctures. He dropped his rifle and grabbed the thorned stalks with his hand, then screamed in agony. Blood trickled into one of his eyes, blinding him while Virgil and Keller both dove for the free rifle.

Priscilla cried and the horses whinnied in terror.

Still blinded and suddenly panicked, Long grabbed for the revolver at his side, but the pistol snagged on the leather thong hooked over the hammer to keep the weapon in place. Long cursed.

As Virgil grabbed the rifle in his throbbing hands, Keller jerked it away from him and hurriedly fired.

The bullet missed, striking the rock and ricocheting around the hiding spot.

Keller squeezed off another shot, which caught Long in the leg. Long cried like a wounded panther and lunged for Keller, tackling him at the knees. As Keller fell to the ground, the rifle flew from his arms toward the pool of water.

Long and Keller rolled in a ball of fury as they tried to beat one another with their fists.

Virgil jumped for the rifle and grabbed it, then cursed as his grip on the stock drove a thorn deeper into his palm. He clenched his jaw against the pain and aimed his rifle at the two men rolling on the ground for advantage.

Long pinned Keller, but just as Virgil was about to pull the trigger Keller pushed him off and Virgil lifted the gun for fear of killing Priscilla's father.

Virgil raised the gun in the air and fired at the sky. "Stop it, Long. It's over."

The two men, their energy sapped by the exertion, eased off. Then, in one final desperate attempt at escape, Long lunged for Virgil's legs.

"Watch out," Priscilla screamed.

Virgil jumped aside and fired, striking Long in the shoulder.

Long cursed again and collapsed, leaking blood from his shoulder and leg now. He struggled to get to his hands and knees, then fell flat, writhing in pain.

Keller jumped up and charged Virgil, ripping the rifle from his hands.

Virgil fell back, fearing Keller would turn on him.

"No," yelled Priscilla.

Keller lifted the rifle to do business, then turned the weapon upon the dying Tom Long. The basin's rock walls echoed with shot after successive shot until Tom Long moved only from the impact of each bullet as it thudded into him.

When the rifle was empty, Keller kept firing, the rifle clicking harmlessly at the dead man. "That's what you get, you bastard, for killing my Connie." Keller stood in a blind rage, yelling at the corpse. Then he took the rifle and clubbed it against the ground and the rock walls until the stock shattered and the metal was scratched and dented. He flung the rifle out of the pit.

For a moment both Keller and Virgil stood still and silent, paralyzed as their brains tried to sort out all that had happened in an instant of time.

Finally, Priscilla's sobs brought them back to the moment. "Please, somebody untie me."

Virgil stepped her way, but Keller charged past him, as if he did not want Virgil to have the opportunity to do anything that might endear him to Priscilla.

"It's okay," he said as he began to unknot the rope around her wrists.

"I feared you'd die, both of you," she sobbed.

Virgil looked at his throbbing hands and began to pull the thorns from them. When he looked up, he saw Priscilla hug her father, then free herself from him. She ran to Virgil, softly taking his hands and starting to remove the thorns.

"Let's get out of here, Prissy," Keller commanded, "before the bad heat sets in."

"No," she answered, "not until I'm done with Virgil. Then we'll all leave together."

"Don't back-talk me, Prissy!"

"I've asked you not to call me that," she replied, never lifting her gaze from Virgil's injured hand.

Keller scowled at Virgil. "Child, I told you I wasn't sure if I would kill to keep the mine."

"You would. I'd already decided that."

Keller nodded. "And, I'd kill to keep someone from taking Priscilla. They already took my Connie. I'm not letting them take Priscilla."

Virgil winced as she pulled the last thorn free. Then Priscilla turned to her father.

"I'm not a horse, something you can keep or trade, depending upon your whims."

Keller puffed out his chest. "Nobody said you were, but you are my daughter."

"I'm eighteen. I'm not yours forever."

Keller growled. "Just get finished with him and let's get out of here. Damn his hide anyway."

Virgil noticed Priscilla's eyes welling with tears. When she lifted her hands to dab at them, he saw rope burns on her wrists. He took her hands, lifting them to his dry lips and kissing them.

She smiled.

"Keep your hands off her, Child," Keller yelled.

In defiance, Virgil escorted her to the pool of water.

She knelt on the stone floor and washed her face and hands. Virgil squatted beside her, washing the blood from his hands, then bent on all fours to drink the water. It was warm and had an odd taste to it, but it was better than he had expected to find anywhere in this petrified hell.

Though Keller stood behind him, Virgil felt safe with Priscilla beside him, and when he arose, she stood up with him.

"Oh, the hell with it," Keller said. "You two take your time. I'll go get our mounts, Child."

His sudden change of heart struck Virgil as odd, especially since his face was as hard as it had been a moment before.

"You help Prissy with her horse," he commanded.

"What about Long?" Virgil asked. "Do you want to take him back to White Oaks?"

"I don't," Keller said. "Let the son of a bitch rot out here."

Virgil nodded.

Keller disappeared up the passageway atop the malpais and Virgil moved to the two horses, which Long had apparently left saddled all night. Virgil unhobbled them and took their reins to lead them toward Priscilla, but both animals balked at passing Long's body.

Virgil motioned for Priscilla to hold the reins. She took them from him and patted the horses on their necks. Then Virgil grabbed Long's boots and pulled him toward the far side of the stone hideout.

The corpse left a trail of blood in its wake. Virgil looked at the corpse and saw Long's sidearm hooked in its holster.

Then it hit him. The guns!

Keller had been going not for the horses, but for the guns that Long had forced them to surrender when he took them captives. Virgil cursed and took a half step toward the passage when he saw Keller standing there with pistol in hand, his grin wider than a crescent moon.

For a moment Priscilla did not understand why Virgil had frozen. Then she looked to the passageway and caught her breath.

"No, no," she screamed. "Don't shoot him."

Keller had a wild look bout him and seemed unable to hear her or care what she said.

Virgil spoke. "I should've known you were going for the guns instead of the horses."

Keller grinned. "It's why I'll die rich and you'll die poor."

"Don't do this, Father. It won't bring Mother back."

"Shut up, Prissy. I don't want any more lip from you. Now lead the horses out of this hole in the ground. It'll be Child's grave too."

"No," she answered defiantly, starting to

270

move toward Keller.

Keller lifted the gun in the air and fired, the rock den exploding with the noise. Priscilla froze in her tracks.

"Do as I said, Prissy."

Priscilla gave Virgil a helpless look.

"Do what he says," Virgil said, eyeing Long's holstered pistol.

She nodded grimly and led the horses past her father. Shortly she and the animals disappeared above.

Virgil squatted, figuring to make himself a smaller target and to edge closer to Long's pistol.

"That's right, you son of a bitch, why don't you crawl?"

Keller laughed as Virgil dropped down on hands and knees and brushed against Long's gun belt, pushing the leather catch off the end of the hammer.

"You're a fool, Child, thinking you could beat a man with money. I'll still be rich and you'll be as dead as your parents."

"You sound like Long, and he's dead now. He was stupid."

Keller lifted the gun upright as he cocked the hammer.

Instantly, Virgil twisted around and jerked the revolver from Long's holster, then rolled over the body as Keller fired.

Up above, he heard Priscilla scream.

He swung his pistol toward Keller, snapping off two quick shots before Keller could move again. Keller looked bewildered, glancing from the holes in his chest to Virgil, then back again. His revolver fell from his hand and he staggered forward, then tumbled to the ground.

Virgil heard the sound of Priscilla's footfall as she ran down the passage. She burst into view, carrying a carbine. "For you," she screamed, pitching it to Virgil, then collapsing in anguish on the ground beside her father.

Virgil caught the carbine with one hand, then shook his head. He knew Keller was dead. There was nothing he could do.

Priscilla looked up from her father's body, her gaze as bewildered as Keller's had been a moment before, then started sobbing.

Dropping Long's pistol on the ground, Virgil stepped tentatively to Priscilla, then helped her up and put his arms around her. She neither encouraged nor resisted his gesture, just cried from the shock. Giving her the carbine, he pointed her to the passage, then picked up Keller's body and toted him atop the malpais. There he tied him to Long's skittish horse.

He helped Priscilla climb aboard her

horse, then picked up his weapons, which were still on the ground where he had dropped them. Then, he started moving cautiously back to his mule and Keller's black gelding.

Beneath his feet the malpais was turning hot, and he was glad to reach the mule and gelding. Without a word, he unhobbled the two animals, tied the gelding behind his mule, then mounted and started back for White Oaks.

Not a dozen words passed between them on the return trip, and it was almost sundown when they rode into the mining town. Virgil shook his head. It was like the first time he had entered White Oaks, escorting a body. Word seemed to have preceded him and people lined the street as he led the string of horses and Priscilla toward the marshal's office.

Someone darted inside and Marshal Nap Webb burst out the door and ran down the street to meet them. He nodded at Virgil, then spoke to Priscilla. "You okay, ma'am?"

"I've been better."

Webb walked over to the body and confirmed it was Ed Keller.

"Sorry about your pa, ma'am."

"Where's Tom Long?"

"Dead on the malpais," Virgil answered.

Webb nodded. "Who killed him?"

"Keller and I did."

The marshal stared at Priscilla. "Who killed your father?"

Virgil wondered what she would say.

Priscilla looked from Webb to Virgil.

"Don't let Child threaten you, ma'am. We're here to protect you. Tell us who killed your pa."

Priscilla's gaze never wavered from Webb.

"Tom Long killed him two years ago, but today's when he died."

23

The line of mourners offering condolences to Priscilla Keller finally reached a trickle as folks returned to their horses and buggies for the short ride back to White Oaks.

Tyrone Weatherby sidled up to Virgil Child. "More folks here than I was expecting, but just a little more than half that attended for his wife."

Virgil looked from the giant stone that marked the Keller grave site to the two temporary wooden markers over his mother's grave.

"It's good they can be buried side by side," Virgil replied.

As the crowd cleared away, Weatherby moved toward the coffin and signaled for a couple hired men in ill-fitting suits to lower the body of Ed Keller into the ground.

A couple women and Keller's Mexican housekeeper lingered with Priscilla. Virgil waited for them to leave, but it didn't seem they were ever going to move, so he ambled toward Priscilla. His hat in his hand, he didn't know quite what to say other than good-bye.

When she saw him, the corner of her lips and her chin lifted.

Virgil was pleased. They hadn't had a chance to talk since they had returned from the malpais.

Priscilla excused herself from the women and walked bashfully toward him.

Virgil straightened the lapels of the same suit he had worn to his mother's funeral.

As she approached, he offered her his hand, but she spurned it and walked into his arms, hugging him and leaning her head against his chest. "I feared you had left White Oaks."

He shook his head. "Not without saying good-bye. You've had enough to worry about the last few days."

"What'll you do?"

"Go back to El Paso and my freight business."

"You have a girl back there?"

He shook his head. "Only one girl I ever gave a second thought, but she doesn't live in El Paso."

"Where does she live?"

Virgil gently pushed Priscilla away from

his chest so he could take in the view of her soft, pale skin, her green eyes and her red hair. "She lives in White Oaks."

Priscilla smiled. "Then why don't you stay?"

Virgil sighed. "I figured she could never forget that it was me that killed her father."

She bit her lip, then whispered softly, "She can't forget, but she can forgive."

Virgil nodded. "Folks would just see me trying to take your money."

Priscilla laughed. "My father's body wasn't even in the grave before some men started trying that. You're decent, Virgil. I knew that the day I first saw you and learned you'd come all the way from El Paso to bury your mother. That kind of son would make a decent husband."

Priscilla blushed at the mention of the word *husband*. "You must think me quite forward, and I admit it's sudden, but once you leave I might never see you again."

Virgil stroked her hair with his fingers, uncertain what to say.

"I'm eighteen," Priscilla said, "and now I own a producing gold mine. You don't think there will be men flocking after me now? I'm smart enough to know I don't know everything. I need someone I can trust, and I know you're an honest man."

Virgil hesitated. He was surprised — but pleased — that she wanted anything to do with him after he'd killed her father.

"You could start your freight line in the territory. If we married, the gold claim that started out in your family's hands would return there."

Still Virgil hesitated. He didn't know why, just that he had to give it a little more thought.

"I think it would be fun."

"What?"

She smiled. "To marry you and grow old and still be a Child."

Virgil saw tears streaming from her eyes.

"Please," she begged, "just consider staying."

Virgil reached in his pocket and pulled out a handkerchief. He dabbed it at the corner of her eyes, then realized it was a bloodstained handkerchief with three names written upon it. He grimaced. "I'm sorry."

She waved her hand to say it didn't matter.

"Come with me," he said, taking her by the hand and escorting her to her father's grave, where Weatherby and his helpers had picked up spades to start covering the coffin.

Priscilla seemed lost for a moment as she

stared at the dirt being dumped on her father's coffin.

Virgil took the bloodstained handkerchief, wadded it up and tossed it into the grave where it disappeared beneath a shovelful of dirt.

Priscilla looked up into his eyes. "Does that mean you will stay?"

Virgil nodded.

Priscilla buried her head against his chest and began to cry, but these tears were unlike any Virgil had ever seen from a woman. They were tears of happiness, and he liked them.

ABOUT THE AUTHOR

Preston Lewis is the Spur Award–winning author of 35-plus novels. He has received two Spur Awards from Western Writers of America (WWA) and a Will Rogers Gold Medallion for Western Humor for *Bluster's Last Stand,* a volume in his comic western series *The Memoirs of H.H. Lomax.* Two Lomax books were Spur finalists. He has earned three Elmer Kelton Awards from the West Texas Historical Association (WTHA) for best creative work on the region.

In 2021 Lewis was inducted into the Texas Institute of Letters for literary accomplishments. A past president of WWA and WTHA, he resides in San Angelo, Texas, with his wife, Harriet. He holds degrees in journalism from Baylor and Ohio State, and a master's degree in history from Angelo State.

The employees of Thorndike Press hope you have enjoyed this Large Print book. All our Thorndike, Wheeler, and Kennebec Large Print titles are designed for easy reading, and all our books are made to last. Other Thorndike Press Large Print books are available at your library, through selected bookstores, or directly from us.

For information about titles, please call:

(800) 223-1244

or visit our website at:

gale.com/thorndike

To share your comments, please write:

Publisher
Thorndike Press
10 Water St., Suite 310
Waterville, ME 04901